Praise for Lucy Monroe:

"If you are a fan of Diana Palmer's, like I am, you definitely need to give Lucy Monroe a try."

—*www.thebestreviews.com*

"*The Sicilian's Marriage Arrangement* is one of those stories that I couldn't wait to finish, but already started to miss when I turned the last page."

—*www.romancejunkies.com*

"Lucy Monroe's books leave me with the 'knowledge that dreams really can come true...'"

—*Fallen Angel Reviews*

Legally wed,
But he's never said...
"I love you"

They're...

The series where marriages are
made in haste...and love comes later....

Look out for more WEDLOCKED! wedding
stories available only from Harlequin Presents®

Coming in November 2005
The Greek's Bought Wife
by Helen Bianchin
#2501

Coming in December 2005
His Wedding-Night Heir
by Sara Craven
#2509

Lucy Monroe

BLACKMAILED INTO MARRIAGE

Wedlocked!

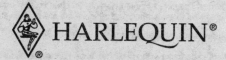

TORONTO • NEW YORK • LONDON
AMSTERDAM • PARIS • SYDNEY • HAMBURG
STOCKHOLM • ATHENS • TOKYO • MILAN • MADRID
PRAGUE • WARSAW • BUDAPEST • AUCKLAND

In memory of my dear friend and fellow writer,
Paulette Jerrells, and with much love for the rest of our
chapter, Olympia RWA. Many thanks for taking this
amazing journey with me.

ISBN 0-373-12484-8

BLACKMAILED INTO MARRIAGE

First North American Publication 2005.

www.eHarlequin.com

Printed in U.S.A.

CHAPTER ONE

"YOU are Rosalia Chavez-Torres."

Lia turned at the deep, masculine voice and found her line of vision blocked by a well-honed male torso clothed in formal black and white. He was standing much too close. She could smell his expensive cologne and powerful energy radiated off him in imposing waves. She took a quick, jerky step backward only to run into a small table that prevented further retreat.

She tilted her head back so her gaze could travel up to the man's face and the breath rushed from her chest.

This man did not belong in a room filled with civilized businessmen.

Oh, he was dressed as the others in a hand-tailored tuxedo that fit his tall, muscular body perfectly. However his eyes burned with a vibrant intensity lacking in the other men in the room. Even her grandfather's presence paled beside this man.

She was absolutely certain he was not old money, nor did she recognize him as a member of the Spanish nobility her grandfather counted among his cronies. She was pretty sure she had met all the eligible men of her age in that circle six years ago…before she'd turned her back on a world she hadn't wanted to belong to. She didn't know *who* he was, but he'd been watching her all evening and it did strange things to her equilibrium. Impossible things she had long ago decided she was not destined to feel.

All of this ran through her mind in the short silent moments after she turned around. Still, his eyes asked why she had not yet responded.

Giving herself a mental shake, she stuck her hand out and said, "Lia Kennedy, actually. And you are?"

"Damian Marquez. You are Benedicto's granddaughter, are you not?" His fingers closed around hers, the heat in them warming hers.

"Yes."

His hands weren't those of a man who had never labored. They were rougher, like Toby's hands had been. Only her husband had been a classic laid-back beta male. Damian exuded an aura of power and hardness that made her already chilled body shiver convulsively.

"You are cold?"

"The air-conditioning…" She let her voice trail off, knowing the AC had nothing to do with it.

Neither did he really. She'd been cold from the inside out since the doctor told her about the hole in her daughter's heart. Returning to Spain and a grandfather who disapproved of all her life's choices had done nothing to warm her.

"We could step onto the terrace. It is still quite warm outside."

She shrugged. Why not? Her grandfather wasn't going to listen to her plea about Kaylee with all these other people around and the prospect of escape was too good to pass up. She hadn't been to his villa on the eastern coast of Spain since Christmas and hadn't been expected until the holiday rolled around next year.

The curiosity of the other dinner guests had been pressing in on her since she walked into the drawing room just as dinner was announced an hour and a half ago. Once dinner had ended and the guests started to mingle, it had become almost unbearable in her current fragile state. If the other guests weren't asking subtly worded questions trying to draw out the reason for her unexpected visit, they were watching her and whispering behind their hands about the too independent granddaughter who was such a disappointment to the old man.

Taking her acquiescence for granted, Damian took her arm and led her through a set of French doors at one end of the long drawing room.

He had been right. The night air was warmer than the chilled interior of the house.

She breathed deeply, enjoying the sensation of heated air caressing her body and filling her lungs. She'd been cold for so long. "This is much better, thank you."

"Most Americans prefer the air-conditioning, but then you grew up here."

"Actually I was raised in the States until I was fifteen." The year her father had died.

The Conde Benedicto Chavez-Torres had insisted Maria-Amelia return to Spain to live with her teenage daughter and Lia's mother had moved across the ocean without a single protest. Sunk in grief over the loss of her husband, she had not noticed how miserable her daughter was in their new home.

She had rejected every concern Lia had voiced, telling her daughter she needed to learn to live with the Spanish side of her nature. Lia hadn't wanted to live in the rarified atmosphere of the wealthy Spanish nobility. She had simply wanted to go home, a request denied time and again by her grandfather.

It should have been no surprise to anyone when she'd eloped with her high school sweetheart at the age of eighteen. Despite the fact their relationship had been long distance for the better part of three years, Toby had expressed more loving understanding toward Lia than either her mother or her grandfather had over those same three years. Yet, both Maria and Benedicto had been furiously shocked by Lia's marriage.

Her grandfather had immediately disinherited her and then been appalled when his action had done nothing to bring her crawling back to Spain. Nothing had done that, not his disapproval, nor her mother's tears and not even Toby's death. Kaylee's illness was another matter.

Lia would do anything for her daughter. Anything at all.

Ignoring the pain her thoughts caused, she added, "I make my home in New Mexico now. It's hot and I like it."

"I see." His dark gaze fixed on her meditatively. "I live in New York. It is hot in the summers, but the winters are very cold."

"Poor you. I would hate to live anywhere with a real winter."

"Perhaps you could learn to like it."

"I don't think so."

He didn't reply immediately and she got the distinct impression he was sizing her up. "Your grandfather said you do not visit Spain very often. I doubt it is the air-conditioning keeping you away."

"My daughter and I come at Christmas every year," she said defensively, not knowing why she should feel the need to defend herself, but feeling it all the same.

"Surely you could come more frequently?"

"Frequent travel doesn't fit into my budget."

"Benedicto would pay for you to come."

She shrugged. No doubt, but then she would have to spend yet more time listening to his lectures about moving to Spain and her mother's more subtle guilt trips. No thank you.

"Perhaps you are so dismissive of your family because you have never had to live without them." Damian's tone was disapproving. Not only did that surprise her—why should he care how close she was to her family—but it also got her back up.

"Tell me something, do you live with *your* parents?"

"My parents are both dead."

"I'm sorry. Losing a parent is devastating, losing both must have been an incredible blow."

"Yes."

His ready agreement surprised her. She had expected him to do the macho, nothing hurts me routine.

"What about your grandparents?" she asked, not willing to concede the point so quickly.

"Neither set recognizes my existence."

All her irritation at his high-handed questioning drained away. "Idiots."

She'd seen that kind of obtuse behavior among her

mother and grandfather's friends and it always made her angry. Her own family had done a fair job of snubbing Toby for the three brief years of her marriage. Her grandfather hadn't even warmed up to Kaylee completely until after Toby had died. Even so he had never tried to completely ignore her existence.

Lia's mother hadn't been so hard, but neither had she made the smallest attempt to make Toby feel like a welcome member of the Chavez-Torres family.

Damian's lips tilted in a half smile. "That is one way to look at it." Benedicto's granddaughter was not shy about speaking her mind. He approved.

He had no desire to marry a doormat, or breed such a character trait into his children.

"It's the only way to look at it. You asked me if family was important to me."

"*Sí,* and you told me that it was." Though clearly not as important as it was to Benedicto.

"*It is,*" she stressed, her amber eyes dark with sincerity. "I could never dismiss my daughter's choice of a husband as a person not worthy of respect and affection just because he wasn't the one I'd chosen for her and no way will I ever reject Kaylee's children because I don't agree with her choices."

His own mother's parents had not felt the same and his father's parents had never once acknowledged the familial connection. He had spent too many years on the outside of a world that should have been his by right of birth. Benedicto Chavez-Torres had helped Damian change that. The help he had given the older man since then had been a small enough price to pay for the vindication of his pride.

"That is not the usual attitude among the people in our world," he said to Lia.

"This world…" She swung her hand out to indicate her grandfather's villa and what it represented. "Is not *my* world. This is my mother and my grandfather's world and I only share it with them because I love them. I prefer the world my daughter and I inhabit in New Mexico."

"Do you?" Or was she making the best of things because her grandfather had disinherited her when she'd married against his advice?

Yet she had made no move to ingratiate herself again, at least not one that had not been of her own choosing. She did not even call herself by her grandfather's name now that both her father and husband were dead. She had to know it would have pleased Benedicto a great deal if she had changed her name back.

Independent. Rosalia Kennedy was very independent, but was she really as uninterested in her grandfather's world and the life of luxury inherent in it as she implied? The terms of the deal Benedicto had proposed said not.

Something of his doubts must have shown on his face because she frowned. "You're very cynical, aren't you?"

A bark of laughter surprised him. Not only independent, but refreshingly frank, not to mention discerning. He was cynical. Life had ensured he became that way. "And you are very forthright."

"More than I should be, probably."

He moved closer to her, invading her space and watching with interest as the pulse at the base of her throat began to beat more rapidly. "I like it."

"Grandfather doesn't." Her breathless voice caressed him like the hand of a very skilled lover.

How much had she learned in three years married to a man who was little more than a boy? Remembering his own sexual knowledge at the age of eighteen, he conceded she might be less innocent than she appeared. However, she was blushing like a virgin and he was not even touching her.

"You are nervous."

"Most women would be around you."

Again he laughed, delighted by her honesty. "Do you know, Rosalia, I believe I like you?"

She tipped her head back so their eyes met squarely. "You sound like that really surprises you."

"It does." He took another step forward, wanting to taste the lips she bit in her agitation.

She retreated, almost stumbling in her haste to get away, but the terrace railing stopped her and he made no effort to allay her obvious discomfort by backing up. Her reaction fascinated him. Women did not usually retreat when he moved forward. They met him with open arms, but hers were crossed defensively over her generous curves.

He wanted to know why. Was she playing a deep game, or was she genuinely nervous around him? He was, after all, still a stranger to her.

She clearly didn't remember the two occasions they had met six years ago, and if she did, he doubted she would have been reassured. He'd made her nervous then, too. She'd been so beautiful she had made him ache with desire, but she'd been too young for what he had wanted from her. Not quite eighteen, she had been strictly off-limits to a man of twenty-three and he had done his best to forget his mentor's granddaughter.

But he had not forgotten.

He wanted her and her current situation dictated that he would have her.

"Rosalia, are you out here?"

Damian moved away, not willing to openly acknowledge his desire for Lia. It would be leverage for Benedicto. While Damian trusted the older man more than anyone else in his life, he had not made tycoon status at such a young age by revealing his weaknesses to anyone. Besides, there was more to this deal than passion and he had a week to decide whether or not he would agree to Benedicto's proposition.

Benedicto's leverage was sadly lacking in this game.

"She is indeed here, Benedicto. We have been getting to know one another."

The older man surveyed Lia and Damian keenly. "And have you learned much of her?"

"Not as much as I would like," he said honestly.

"Ah, this is good." Benedicto smiled.

Lia blushed again and averted her face.

"And you, Rosalia, do you enjoy the company of my friend?"

Lia's head came up and she searched her grandfather's eyes, her own starkly vulnerable. "I thought he was a business associate."

"That, too. We have known each other many years."

"I see. Grandfather, I need to speak to you. Kaylee—"

"Not now, Rosalia." The harshness of Benedicto's tone shocked Damian.

Even more unexpected…anger welled up at the way

the words made Lia flinch. "I am happy to leave you two in privacy," he said in a tone he knew Benedicto would not mistake.

Indeed the old man's face tightened and his eyes said he recognized the warning. However, he shook his head. "Nonsense. The terrace during a dinner party is hardly the place for the conversation my granddaughter wishes to have. Is that not true, Rosalia?"

She looked like she wanted to argue, but she nodded instead. Then she sighed as if acceding with more than mere words. "Yes, Grandfather. You are right." She stepped away from the terrace railing. "That being the case, however, I think I'll say goodnight. I'm still adjusting to the time change."

She stopped speaking, her body held in tension as if she was waiting for Benedicto to react.

He smiled again, the warmth in his eyes unmistakable to Damian, but he got the impression Lia did not see it. "Sleep well, Rosalia."

"I will see you tomorrow," Damian promised.

"Tomorrow?" she asked uncertainly.

"Damian is staying with us."

"Oh. Goodnight then." She turned and fled. There was no other description for her hasty exit.

"Your granddaughter is shy," Damian remarked as the silence stretched between him and the first person to believe in him enough to invest in a Marquez, Ltd. venture.

"She will make an admirable wife. You will not find her flirting with the waitstaff in the kitchen during one of your parties."

The reminder of one of the less than pleasant memories he shared with Benedicto routed the softened feelings he had allowed to creep in while talking to Lia. It was exactly memories like that one that had made him listen to Benedicto in the first place when the old man had come to Damian with his proposal.

Marry Lia and be guaranteed at least half of the Chavez-Torres business holdings. While the collapse of the world's stock market had dictated that Benedicto's fortune was not what it once was, his holdings had more value than mere money. They represented a foothold in business interests usually reserved for the Spanish nobility. Damian's pride demanded more than undeniable wealth, he wanted what the illegitimacy of his birth had denied him.

Acceptance. Even if it was forced. He would sit on the boards of several companies with his younger brother, the only legitimate son to their father and their sister as well, the holder of the title that should have been his.

Another reason Benedicto's proposal had been so palatable. Under a special dispensation from the king, the Conde was prepared to cede one of his lesser titles to Damian once he became a member by marriage of the Chavez-Torres family. All of his other titles would pass eventually to his granddaughter and ultimately to Damian's own children.

It would require Lia and her grandfather signing documents to the effect that Kaylee Kennedy, an American citizen, would not inherit the titles from her Spanish family. According to Benedicto, Lia would be more than willing for such a passage of events. And if her earlier words were to be believed at all, Damian suspected the old man was right.

The next morning, Lia saw Damian at breakfast, just as he had promised the night before, but her grandfather was nowhere in sight.

"He had a business meeting," Maria-Amelia said from the other side of the table. "He told Rosa not to expect him back in time for dinner."

Dinner? "What about lunch?"

"We are meeting associates in Alicante," Damian said, his demeanor that of the hard-bitten businessman again.

She had thought last night he had relaxed with her, but she must have been mistaken. She certainly hadn't been thinking straight, or she would not have let him get so close. She was almost positive he would have kissed her if Grandfather had not interrupted. For once, she was grateful for his interference.

"Perhaps you would like to join me on a shopping trip?" Lia's mother asked.

Lia smiled, knowing it was her mother's way of getting her mind off of her problems. She accepted, more for the chance to distance herself from Damian's disturbing presence, than any hope shopping could keep her from worrying about Kaylee's future.

That night, as she tucked her daughter into bed, Lia found it very difficult to believe the small, blond pixie-faced girl looking up at her had something as serious as a hole in her heart. Her blue eyes clear with child-like innocence and her skin a soft, healthy pink, she didn't look in the least bit sick.

But looks could be deceiving when it came to a genetic defect like the one Kaylee carried, as the heart specialist had taken pains to point out to her.

"Mama, are you sad?"

Lia smiled, concentrating on projecting the love that had filled her soul since the moment she'd learned she carried her daughter. "I'm fine, sweetheart. How about you? All recovered from the plane ride?"

Kaylee grinned, but then covered her mouth with a small hand as she yawned. "I love flying, silly."

"It's a good thing since your grandmother and great-grandfather live so far away."

"Abuela Maria-Amelia must not like to fly because she never comes to see us."

Lia leaned down and kissed her daughter's cheek. Her mother's lack of visits had a lot more to do with the humble way Lia and Kaylee lived than discomfort on a plane. She didn't say that however. Her daughter would not understand and Lia never wanted Kaylee to feel rejected by her family. Not as she had been.

"That must be it. I can't imagine anyone not wanting to see lots and lots of a sweet girl like you otherwise."

Kaylee giggled. "I love you, Mama."

"I love you, too, butterfly." Lia finished tucking her daughter in, making sure the blanket was snug around her small body.

Grandfather really did keep the house rather chilly.

She stood up to go. Stopping at the door, she turned off the light and then looked back over her shoulder to say goodnight one last time. Kaylee's eyelids were already drooping.

"Mama?"

"Yes, sweetheart?"

"I met a nice man today."

"You did? When?"

"You were gone with *Abuela* and he came outside to watch me skip rope." The doctor had said that mild exercise should not be a problem for Kaylee…not yet. "He counted skips with me."

"Who was it?"

"Damian. He said he was your friend."

Damian had watched her daughter play? The concept shocked her, but she found herself smiling. "A *new* friend."

"He's my new friend, too."

"And I am a very lucky man to have made two such lovely friends in less than two days." Damian's voice from directly behind her shocked Lia into whirling around.

"What are you doing here?"

"I hoped to be early enough to say goodnight to Kaylee."

"Oh." Nonplussed, she didn't know what else to say, but her daughter was not so reticent.

"Damian!" She sat straight up in bed, her tiredness disappearing as if it had never been. "I want a hug."

Lia knew there was nothing for it but to turn the light back on and allow the big man to say goodnight to her small daughter. He did so, easily cajoled into reading Kaylee a second bedtime story. Lia had read her the first one. It was all so unreal that Lia spent the next fifteen minutes in a complete daze. This was simply not a side of the powerful executive she had expected to see.

Even more shocking was the effect his proximity had on *her. She was attracted to him.* For a woman with her past, that was more than amazing, it was unbelievable and yet even she could not misread the way her heart raced and breath went short when he was near. She wanted to touch him and that scared her to death.

While her grandfather seemed intent on avoiding her over the next couple of days, Damian was always there. He drew her like an irresistible force and he didn't seem to mind at all. No doubt he was staying with her grandfather for business purposes, but he spent more time with her and Kaylee. Neither Benedicto nor Maria seemed taken aback by this state of affairs.

Despite her growing concern on her daughter's behalf—why had her grandfather refused to make time to talk to her—Lia enjoyed her time in Damian's company. They had a lot in common and merely being in the same room with him sent a sensual charge zinging straight to the core of her. The feeling was so remarkable that even if he hadn't returned the attraction, she would have found it impossible to stay away.

However, he made it clear in one subtle way after another that he saw her as a desirable woman and his desire fanned her own in ways she found both confusing and frightening.

Damian Marquez was a master tactician and true to the nature she had first sensed in him, he entered a battle to win it. She had the distinct impression he saw her as the spoils of victory. Toby could have told him that when it came to sex, she was more likely to spoil the victory than enhance it. And yet, despite her past and what she knew of her own body, Damian succeeded in seducing her latent sensuality to life.

It had been so long since she felt anything like it, she'd forgotten what it meant to be a woman and the reminder added to her already charged emotions. Something had to give soon, or she was going to fly apart at the seams from everything tearing at her.

She needed to know her daughter was going to be okay. Every passing day increased her fear for Kaylee's future. As inconceivable as she found it, she could not shake the worry her grandfather was avoiding her because he was going to refuse help.

Desperation clawed at her insides with growing ferocity until she felt like her emotions were the powder inside a stick of dynamite with a short fuse.

And Damian was the fire that would light it, blowing apart her world and her ability to deal with everything happening to her. She urgently needed to get away from him before she did something unutterably stupid, like try to act on the feelings he aroused in her.

CHAPTER TWO

LIA was once again outside, hoping the warm summer evening would dispel some of the chill her grandfather's latest refusal to speak to her had left inside her chest. He hadn't actually come out and said he would not speak to her, but he'd made it clear he and Damian had business to discuss after dinner. Lia wanted to tell him to stuff his business, but what good would that do?

And it could do a great deal of harm for Kaylee. No matter what it took, she had to get the money for Kaylee's surgery, even if it meant swallowing her anger along with her pride. She would beg if that was what it took, but she *needed* her grandfather's help. She'd run out of other options before ever coming to Spain.

The insurance company had denied her claim based on the "preexisting condition" clause. Lia still fumed when she thought of that stupid doctor who had said Kaylee's abnormal test results were nothing to worry about when she was a baby. This was the same doctor who had told her to drink a glass of wine before sex and everything would be fine.

He'd been wrong about that, too.

The test results had indicated a hole in Kaylee's heart that would only get worse as she got older. While the risk of heart attack or stroke was extremely low, *it was there* and if the condition wasn't fixed…that risk would increase with each passing year.

Toby's parents would have given the money if they could, but they had had their son late in life and were living on a small, fixed retirement income. They'd offered to sell their two-bedroom house in the New Mexico desert, but the truth was, even if they gave her all the proceeds, it still wouldn't have been enough. And Lia's income as a nursery school teacher barely covered the necessities of life. It certainly left nothing over to save for a possible disaster, medical or otherwise.

Lia sighed, curling her legs onto the bench. Even with the cushion, the stone surface wasn't exactly comfortable, but she didn't mind. At least she was alone with her thoughts. A soft breeze on the warm evening air-brushed her skin, reminding her that she was still capable of enjoying physical sensations. Strange how that could be true after all she had been through.

"Are you avoiding the air-conditioning again?"

Startled at the now familiar voice when she thought she was alone, her head jerked up. "Damian."

He stood over her with one eyebrow tilted quizzically. "You appear pensive."

"I am. I need to talk to my grandfather, but he's made himself scarce for three days now. I'm getting desperate." In spite of her disturbing thoughts, Damian's proximity sent frissons of sensation rushing along her nerve endings.

"I am sure he will discuss all the details with you when the time is right."

"You know why I'm here?" she asked, shocked her grandfather would have shared the information.

After all, family business was just that. *Family business* and while it was obvious Damian and her grandfather shared a special rapport, Señor Marquez was not family.

"*Sí*. Benedicto and I have talked a great deal." He sat down beside her, laying his hand across the back of the bench and his fingertips brushed the bare skin of her shoulder.

The small touch sent more tremors through her nervous system and she wished she'd worn a dress that had more to it than her simple black sheath with spaghetti straps. It left her all too vulnerable to such casual caresses.

"Your skin is so soft." His rich, masculine voice did impossible things to her insides while he ran a single fingertip along her collarbone. "*Bonita.*"

He thought her beautiful? She almost laughed. She'd gotten so used to seeing herself as a sexless being, incapable of a woman's pleasure that she'd forgotten men could still find her attractive.

"We shouldn't—"

"Shh…" His fingertips moved to cover her mouth, stopping her protest before it could form. "This is something we must know."

She couldn't form a coherent thought to wonder what he was talking about. It was as if a sorcerer's spell had been cast and she was paralyzed by its enchantment. The still lucid part of her knew she should pull away, but she couldn't make herself do it. The small touch was too intoxicating.

For just this moment in time, she felt connected to another person and she desperately needed that.

She'd been alone so long.

He moved closer until his hard thigh brushed up against hers, his arm coming down to close around her shoulders. "Your grandfather and I were discussing details and I realized there was one thing I had to be sure of before making a final decision. No doubt you are curious, too."

"Curious?"

She wasn't sure he heard her barely whispered question because his mouth was already descending. Had she even spoken it aloud?

"Your voice is very breathy," he said, answering her thoughts. His lips hovered above hers. "Why is that I wonder?"

Warmth unfurled inside her at his teasing tone.

"I find you very attractive," she admitted, knowing even as she said the words, she shouldn't.

He would think she was inviting intimacy and she could not do that, no matter how much she wanted it… but oh how she wanted it.

His nostrils flared. "I am attracted to you too, Lia. This is a good thing."

"I—" She never knew what she would have said because his mouth closed over hers at that moment.

Time stopped.

Sensations she'd never known buffeted her and the world and everything in it ceased to exist…except Damian and what he made her feel.

His mouth moved over hers with expert seduction, drawing her lips into parting slightly so he could barely penetrate her with his tongue. He tasted like the wine they'd had with dinner and something else, something she found far more powerful of an aphrodisiac…himself.

She moaned and grabbed his pristine white shirt with both fists, terrified he would pull away and end the amazing sensations pouring through her. But his lips remained warm and insistent, coaxing her to a response she had not known she was capable of giving.

Her lips parted further of their own accord and Damian's tongue slipped completely inside, laying claim to her mouth with total possession. His mouth said, *You belong to me.*

Her lips responded silently but with unmistakable intent. *Yes, I do.*

And for this moment out of time she did.

Strong, but gentle fingers cupped her breast, jolting her with the intimacy of the action, but even then she could not force herself to pull away, to tell him they had to stop. Even though part of her waited with trepidation for him to grab her roughly and squeeze, she loved the feel of his fingers against her sensitive flesh. Only he didn't grab. His thumb brushed over her nipple, making her groan as the peak tightened with unexpected pleasure.

He pulled her closer against him and she let her hands flatten against the hard muscles of his chest. She shuddered at the contact, unable to believe she was this way with him. Exploring with her fingertips, she traced the bulge of his muscles and the shape of his torso.

Being so close to another person, having the freedom to touch was such a heady sensation, she lost what little remained of her common sense.

His mouth moved to her cheek and down her neck, wreaking havoc with her nerve endings. "Lia, you are driving me crazy."

"I don't mean to," she moaned.

His husky laughter shivered through her like an internal caress. "I do not mind."

"I'm gla…" He bit her earlobe and she lost the ability to speak.

A very tiny voice in the back of her mind told her she had to stop, that she couldn't let this go on. But it was drowned out by the clamoring voice of passion, a voice she had not heard since her wedding night seven years ago. His fingers did something to her nipple that sent her coherent thoughts rocketing to the heavens. She pressed herself into his hand while her own fingers scrabbled with the buttons on his shirt.

She wanted to feel the heat of his skin, just once.

She found the light dusting of hair across his chest unbearably exciting as she brushed through it until she found the hard points of his nipples. She caressed them and his big body shuddered.

"Yes, touch me, *querida*."

She did, lightly pinching them as he had done to her, and he groaned, long and low.

His grip on her waist tightened until she had no hope of movement, but she didn't mind because his lips were slanting over hers again.

When she felt warm air on her breasts, it only vaguely registered. Even the feel of his rough fingers against her bare flesh only filled her with searing desire, none of the fear she'd experienced during sex in her marriage.

His mouth broke away from hers to move to her bourgeoning peak and she dug her fingernails into his chest. When he started suckling, she cried out, and then bit her own hand to keep the moans from coming out.

"You are so responsive. It is amazing."

She wasn't. Not with anyone but him. Her head moved from side to side in a mixture of sexual frenzy and denial, but then his hand slid up inside her thigh. Nerve endings that had gone without stimulus for years flared into life with the power of a flash-fire in a bone-dry forest. The heat between her legs crackled and blazed, searing her with its intensity.

His touch skimmed closer to the heart of her need and a tendril of sanity reached out to wrap around her mind. Memories of her numerous failed attempts at intimacy pressed for recognition, but she refused to give in to them.

Surely it would be all right. She was so excited, her body would admit him. It had to.

But it didn't. He touched her between her legs with just his fingertip and she could feel the spasms, knew her vaginal walls were closing. Soon, he would know, too. He would discover her complete lack of femininity and she could not stand it.

Toby's love had turned to anger and finally pity, but her husband had made one thing very clear. No man wanted a woman incapable of having sex.

She broke away from Damian and surged off the bench, shocking him with her violent rejection.

His body was shaking, the unmistakable bulge of his arousal a testament to what he wanted to do with her.

"Lia. What is it?"

"We can't."

He looked around him, as if he could not believe what he saw. "You are right. Not here. Come to my room."

She shook her head, incapable of vocalizing her rejection, her hands coming up to hide her nudity that now made her feel vulnerable.

Comprehension followed by an expression of pure cynicism washed over his features. "You wish to wait."

"No...you don't understand."

"Ah, but I do." He smiled, though no humor or warmth entered his eyes. "At least my question has been answered. I will finish negotiations with your grandfather."

"You think I did that—" she flailed her hand toward the bench where they had come so close to making love "—so you would negotiate something with my grandfather?"

She felt sick and it wasn't just because her body had once again failed her.

His expression unreadable, Damian looked at her for several seconds and then he shook his head. "No. I believe the passion, it is real. You want me and that is enough. Who am I to complain if you want the deal closed before you are willing to consummate it? It is, after all, how I do business all the time."

She didn't know what he was talking about, but she wasn't hanging around to figure it out. Her emotions were all over the place and it was because of the man who stood there looking and talking as if what had just occurred had been nothing more than a particularly physical form of business negotiations.

She turned and fled without another word.

The sound of her name on his lips only made her walk faster until she was almost running up the stairs to the safety of her bedroom.

Benedicto Chavez-Torres kept his study only slightly warmer than the rest of the house and Lia shivered as she waited for her grandfather to finish his phone call so they could talk.

He hung up the phone and fixed his steely gaze on her across the expanse of his huge mahogany executive desk. "Your mother said you have something you wish to ask me."

There was no point in hedging, so she didn't even try. "I need money, a lot of it."

"For?"

Her heart sank to the pit of her stomach. "Please, let's not play these games, Grandfather. Mother told you about Kaylee and her heart condition. I know she did. And now I need to know whether you will help."

"*Sí*. Your daughter needs surgery, I gather."

"She's your great-granddaughter, too." How could he play this cold game again?

She thought he'd finally accepted Kaylee after Toby died. True, Lia's grandfather hadn't made any extra efforts to get to know his great-granddaughter in the last three years, but he hadn't made any overtures toward Lia, either. It was just his way. He was not a demonstrative man, or so she had always told herself.

"I do not deny the Chavez-Torres blood in her veins. Surely it is you who do that."

"Choosing to live in America is not a denial of my Spanish family."

"That is a matter of interpretation."

She'd been prepared for this. She knew the money would not come without a cost and she was willing to pay it, whatever it was. His first sally was expected and one she actually welcomed.

Moving to Spain to live for the next few months would be the best alternative for Kaylee. Lia could not afford to maintain a separate dwelling without working and she needed to stay home full-time with her daughter to care for her after the surgery.

"Will our moving back to Spain change your attitude?"

"How much money do you need?" her grandfather asked, without answering her question.

She named a sum that covered the surgery, Kaylee's stay in the hospital and basic living expenses for her and Kaylee during the time that Lia would not be able to work. It was an astronomical figure as far as she was concerned, but she knew her grandfather could easily afford it.

"You will receive twice that on two conditions."

"What conditions?" she asked warily.

Her grandfather was a shrewd negotiator and he had long since made it clear he did not approve of Lia's life choices.

"I am an old man now, Rosalia. I have no son to leave my company to. I feel this more deeply as each year passes."

"You have a daughter," she reminded him.

"Your mother has no interest in business."

Lia could not argue that truth. "What has this got to do with Kaylee?"

"Nothing."

"But…"

"It has to do with the conditions I have for gifting you the money you require."

She remained silent, waiting for him to list the conditions.

"I want an heir, someone to leave my company to."

"You want to raise Kaylee here as your heir?" The thought horrified her. Lia's daughter would have no chance to pursue her own dreams in life if she were locked into her grandfather's will.

"You mistake me." He leaned back in his chair and smiled. "It is time you remarried."

Lia gasped, the blood leaching from her face, leaving her skin frigid with cold and her lips stiff. She was never marrying again. She couldn't! *No.*

"Yes." Her grandfather stood and towered over the desk, all pretense of pleasant affability gone. "You mourn your first husband like he was a god. He was but a man and not a great man at that."

She would have stood, too, but she doubted her legs would have supported. "Toby was good to me." In every way but one and that one hadn't been his fault. It was hers.

"He was a boy playing at being a man." Benedicto's lips curled in derision. "He took you from your family, forcing you to live with less than even my servants live with."

"Millions of people the world over live under much worse financial restrictions."

"These millions are not my granddaughter." He was every inch the Spanish nobleman in that moment, his expectation that she would always live as a Chavez-Torres stronger than ever, even if technically she was a Kennedy.

"I'll move back to Spain. I'll even do my best to fit into your and my mother's world, but I will never re-marry."

He looked down his patrician nose at her and she thought, not for the first time, that she knew how peasants had felt in the face of her ancestors hundreds of years ago. "You are in no position to dictate terms. The insurance company has refused to pay for Kaylee's surgery and convalescence and your *other* relatives are in no position to help you."

"Are you sure about that?" She hadn't told her mother about her insurance policy, hoping not to let her grandfather know how desperate she really was.

"Quite sure. A few phone calls after your mother told me of Kaylee's condition and I knew all. Your financial situation is as dire as it can get."

"I'm not exactly living in my car."

"Neither do you own your own home and the small house you rent is a hovel."

"It isn't, but that is not the issue."

"No. The issue is what you are willing to do to guarantee your daughter's future."

She blanched at the cruel ruthlessness of his words. "Are you saying Kaylee's life means nothing to you?"

"You both mean a great deal to me, but I will not pay

to have her heart fixed only to stand by and watch you destroy both yours and her life out of misguided pride and stubbornness."

"You think me remarrying will not do that?"

"I'm sure of it."

"You can't be serious." But he could, his implacable expression said so. "I'm not even dating."

"I do not expect you to find your next husband, in fact, it would no doubt be another disaster if I allowed you to do so. I have selected him for you."

"You've picked out a husband for me?"

"Yes."

"Impossible. Even you aren't such a dinosaur that you believe in arranged marriages."

He shook his head and sat down again, his tanned aristocratic features set in grim lines. "But I do, *niña.* In certain circumstances, they are the only way."

"And you believe this is one of those circumstances?"

"Yes."

"How can you use a child's life as a bargaining chip to get what you want?" She swallowed the bile that filled her throat at his machinations. "I always knew you were hard, but I never thought you were without a conscience."

He shook his head almost wearily, for a moment looking every one of his sixty-eight years. "You have never understood me, *niña,* nor do you truly know me. I do not expect you to begin now. Believe only that if you do not fulfill my conditions, you will not receive the money you have asked for."

"Please, Grandfather. Don't do this."

His expression turned as impassive as a rock, all softness gone as if it had never been. "I have no choice."

"But you do…" Her voice trailed off at the implacable glint in his dark eyes.

They stared at one another, her weighing his resolve, him simply waiting for her to come to terms with it. Or so it seemed to her.

But then he spoke and his voice was laced with unexpected desperation. "Believe me when I tell you, I truly have no choice."

The cracks in the front of his Spanish pride convinced her as no words could do.

"Who have you chosen to fill the exalted role of husband to the granddaughter of Benedicto Chavez-Torres?" she finally asked, unwilling to beg for information he had not offered.

Like why he had no choice and what that meant for her and Kaylee.

"Damian Marquez."

She'd known the man was staying with her grandfather for business, only she *hadn't* known *she* was the business. "You're assuming he will be agreeable?"

"We've already settled on terms."

"Impossible," she said, her voice scratchy with tension.

"No, it is not. Your marriage will be the final contract in a merger that will benefit us both, but I must be honest, myself more than Damian."

He saw marriage between her and his business associate as nothing more than a financial merger? "That is sick."

This sort of thing simply did not happen in this day and age. *Of course it did,* her practical mind contradicted her outraged heart, *just not in the circles you've been living in the last seven years.* Her grandfather would see nothing out of the ordinary in directing her life like this, but it was still so medieval, it should be a historical movie script, not her life.

He merely shrugged as if to say her emotions had no place in his business dealings. "I admire Damian much as I would a son. It is more than good business."

"He's hardly from your class," she broke in bitterly.

"That is a foolish remark and it is not true. His father was a *don,* but his mother was the man's mistress, not his wife. Neither family acknowledges him and that is their loss. Damian is very intelligent, ruthless when he needs to be and he knows how to run a business and make a profit."

He sounded like a carbon copy of her grandfather, especially the *ruthless when he needed to be* part.

"Lia, you need a great deal of money. Due to a reversal of fortune, I am in no place to give you that money. Damian is. I suggested the marriage as a personal seal on a merger between the two of us, a way for him to receive some compensation for the financial help he has given me over the past few years and the help you need now. It is little enough to ask."

"You think marriage is a small price to pay for his help?" she asked, unable to hide her horror at the idea.

Her grandfather ignored it. "He came to stay this week to see if he would be amenable to the marriage and I am happy to say he is."

"You mean he was here to check out the merchandise?" she demanded, knowing she was being crude and not caring.

"Do not speak of yourself this way. It is beneath you." Her grandfather's words of angry disapproval barely registered as a wave of hurt broke over her with drowning force.

She'd liked Damian. How could she have been so stupid? No man in her grandfather's world would have spent the kind of time Damian had with her and Kaylee without an ulterior motive. His had been a business deal.

Funny, she would have thought the man she'd gotten to know over the past few days incapable of blackmailing a woman into marriage, but then he probably didn't see it that way. To him it was no doubt a matter of getting adequate return on his investment. A cold and calculated motive, but not one entirely foreign to her grandfather's world.

Still, she had thought Damian was different. More the fool her. Clearly she was a lousy judge of character.

"He would give you the money if you asked without marriage to me a stipulated condition." She said it in desperation, not at all sure it was true.

Her grandfather shook his head, dashing not even fully formed hopes. "He is a shrewd businessman. He will not give something for nothing. What besides yourself do you have to offer this man for his money?"

"You make me sound like a whore."

"*No.* A whore would become the man's mistress."

A job she was even less qualified for than being a wife.

"You are not selling your body," her grandfather continued in her silence, "you are agreeing to share his life in exchange for your daughter's well-being. And I am not merely discussing her heart condition here, *niña.*"

"You could *try* asking."

"I have no desire to do so. I want you to marry him, Rosalia. Accept that."

"I can't accept that you are willing to use Kaylee's health as blackmail leverage."

"I want more than one granddaughter."

Suddenly she understood. This wasn't just about business, this was about propagating the Chavez-Torres line. "You expect me to give you a grandson with Damian," she whispered in appalled tones Benedicto would not begin to understand.

"Damian is ready to have children. Only God may determine whether one of them is a boy."

"But you'll take the chance so you can get your heir…"

The old man had the temerity to shrug. "Your mother had only you and you have but one child, an American citizen at that…it is not enough to see the continuation of a family line, nor will you raise Kaylee to accept the responsibilities due the title."

He was right, but what difference did that make?

She shook her head, punch-drunk from what he was saying. If only he knew it, he asked the one thing she was totally incapable of giving, even if she'd wanted to.

CHAPTER THREE

"I NEVER want to marry again. *I can't.*"

"Nonsense." His will washed over her like an incoming tide. "You are young. You are fertile."

"Did you make calls regarding that as well?" she asked scathingly.

"I did not have to. Kaylee is proof of your ability to conceive. She was born within a year of your marriage to Tobias Kennedy. While I approve your choice to prevent conception soon after, sufficient time has passed for you to safely become pregnant again."

"Do you even hear yourself? You're not God, Grandfather. You can't dictate life."

"I am a mere man, but one that has what you want more than your freedom I think. You *can* marry and you will."

"What does Damian get out of this?"

"A title. Entrée into a society that has spurned him. The legitimacy he craves."

"I wouldn't think that would matter with a man like him."

"His pride demands recognition where it has been denied."

"He doesn't need an old man arranging his marriage."

"I can give him what few others can."

"What?"

"I will cede a lesser title to him. Your oldest child will inherit a legacy denied him as well *and* he approves of you as a bride."

"Why?"

"He finds you pleasing." When she snorted at that, he went on. "You are a Chavez-Torres. You will not marry him only to divorce him a year hence and take a large settlement with you."

"What's stopping me?"

"Your promise."

"You expect me to promise to stay married to him indefinitely?"

"Yes."

"Absolutely not. That leaves me open to abuse and humiliation because all the power is on his side," she said, a desperate plan forming in her mind. "My promise is only binding as long as he maintains the sanctity of his marriage vows."

"This is to be expected."

"I want it in writing and it must be understood that I will not stay with him if he mistreats me or Kaylee in any way."

"Granted." His tone rang with satisfaction. "However, you will give me your word you will do nothing to undermine the marriage."

"What do you mean?" Her word meant a great deal to her, but not as much as her daughter's life.

"You will respect your vows and you will not attempt

to embarrass or infuriate Damian into ending the marriage."

Relieved, she smiled. "I promise."

She wouldn't have to. When he discovered she was incapable of performing as a woman, he wouldn't be able to get out of the marriage fast enough. Toby had loved her, but even he could not continue with a marriage that included no physical intimacy.

"I want the money transferred into my account the day of my marriage, before I leave the reception."

"That can be arranged, but you realize once you marry Damian, you will have access to more than sufficient funds to care for Kaylee's health concerns."

"That is not part of the bargain. You promised me a certain sum and I don't care who's paying it. I want it in my account that day."

"Very well."

The rest of the negotiations were completed in a matter of minutes.

Damian sipped at his club soda while he and Benedicto waited for Lia to join them. "You know, when you first suggested this arrangement, I was skeptical, Benedicto."

"I could see that you were."

"But your granddaughter is everything you said she would be. Lovely. Charming." Passionate, but that wasn't one of the things the old man had listed when he'd extolled Lia's virtues. Damian had been forced to discover it on his own and the test had been no hardship. He looked forward to his wedding night with a sense of anticipation he had felt for nothing else in a very long time.

"She is a good mother." As his own had been.

Lia was also like his mother in that she was willing to do whatever necessary to make sure Kaylee's life was the best it could be. Benedicto had made no bones about the fact that Lia was willing to agree to the marriage because she wanted to guarantee Kaylee's future.

Damian could respect that.

"She loves her daughter and she will make a fine mother to the children she will give you."

"Your great-grandchildren."

"*Sí*." Benedicto's eyes warmed. "Kaylee is a treasure, but I want to leave behind a legacy, not a single child I hope will pass the blood of my ancestors on to the next generation."

Damian did not scoff at the older man's desires. They matched his own after all. He had worked hard to build a business from nothing, but had realized on his thirtieth birthday that he had no one who truly appreciated his efforts, no children to pass on a birthright that was infinitely better than the one his parents had passed on to him.

Benedicto had suggested marriage to his granddaughter as the solution to both their problems.

It did not bother Damian that Lia proposed to marry him for the security he could give her. It was at least an honest business proposition, not avarice masquerading as love. He'd been down that road, not once, but twice and both times Benedicto had been there not only to point out the truth of the situation, but to support him afterward.

Marriage to the man's granddaughter felt right in a way Damian wasn't sure he understood. It had something to do with feeling like he belonged to a family again, but such considerations were not inner issues he would willingly examine.

The lawyer arrived with his assistant and all personal talk ceased.

"I see everyone is here and I am the last to arrive." The sound of Lia's soft voice had the men surging to their feet.

Damian smiled. "Surely that is a woman's prerogative."

She shrugged gracefully and took the empty chair nearest him. "I suppose, but I'm sorry if I've made you all wait."

"It is nothing," Benedicto dismissed while Damian studied Lia closely.

Her eyes lacked the warmth they had held on the previous occasions they had met and her tone was almost brittle.

"Lia," he said, using the name she'd told him she preferred.

"Yes?"

"Are you certain you want to go through with this?"

Her golden eyes widened and for just a second he saw vulnerability there that kicked at his gut, but then she masked it and smiled. "Yes."

"Do not worry, Damian. My granddaughter would not have given her word if she did not intend to keep it."

"Perhaps she has changed her mind." He did not want a reluctant wife.

Either she was okay with this business proposition, or she wasn't. There was no in-between.

"Have you changed your mind, Rosalia?" Benedicto asked, the words coming out like a challenge.

Her shoulders squared and her kissable mouth firmed in a determined line. "No. I assume *you* are still willing to go through with this merger?" she asked Damian.

"A marriage is much more personal than a merger."

"Yes, it is." The husky softness of her voice impacted his libido like a sledgehammer against a crumbling brick wall.

His usual defenses tumbled in a heartbeat, leaving him aching with a desire he had to wait four weeks to slake.

The lawyer cleared his throat and placed a set of documents on the large desk Benedicto had ceded to him for use during this meeting. "Ms. Kennedy, these papers are for your signature."

She did not move. "I was under the impression we all had papers to sign today."

"Yes, of course, Ms. Kennedy. Your grandfather will sign some of these documents and Señor Marquez as well."

"I see. Ladies first, is that it?"

"It was the *Conde's* wish to sign in this order."

Without another word, Lia leaned forward and began reading the papers. She flipped through the prenuptial agreement with no more than a cursory glance and set it aside. She barely skimmed the agreement ceding any and all rights Kaylee had to the Chavez-Torres titles. She spent a little more time reading the two-page document agreement between the two of them stipulating grounds for the end of their marriage, but she set it aside as well without signing it.

The final document detailed the financial sum that Damian had agreed to settle on her the day of their marriage. He would have been worried if it had been a million dollars, but the few hundred thousand she asked for was hardly enough to justify her reneging on their marriage and taking Kaylee to live on their own on his largesse.

She read the document carefully and then lifted her head. "I want you to sign this before I put my signature on anything else here."

Damian frowned, offended at the lack of trust she appeared to have in his integrity. "I have given my word to sign it as well as the others."

"Then you won't mind signing this one first."

"I mind your implication of mistrust."

She bit her lip and then squared her shoulders. "I'm sorry. Is it really such a big deal, or is this a male pride thing?"

He found his lips twitching in a smile. "You don't think much of the male pride thing?"

"No."

He shook his head and thought marriage to her might be less serene than he had at first anticipated, but he didn't mind. In fact, his blood heated in his veins at the prospect. "Very well." He signed the papers.

Once he was done, Lia put her signature to all three documents without reading them again. Damian had already read the papers, having hammered out the terms with Benedicto earlier in the week. So, he quickly added his signature to hers.

Lia stood up. "I'll leave you gentlemen to your business. I need to pack for my return to New Mexico."

"There is no need," Benedicto said.

"I don't like others packing for me."

"I mean, you have no need to return. We can arrange for your belongings, such as they are, to be shipped to Spain. You are needed here to help your mother with the wedding preparations."

"She doesn't need my help. She has you. I'm sure you've already got the entire event planned down to the last detail." She turned to go, but stopped in the doorway and looked back at Damian, the expression in her amber eyes unreadable. "I will be back in time for the wedding. If you need to contact me, Grandfather has my phone number."

"Lia, this is rid—" Benedicto stopped mid-word because his granddaughter was already gone.

"She's an independent woman, is she not?" Damian asked.

"Sí." Benedicto sighed. "Too independent."

"Does she really intend to leave the entire wedding planning to you and Maria-Amelia?"

"I'm afraid so."

"Well, Lia may not have any ideas for our wedding, but I do. I do not want any plans made without my approval."

Benedicto laughed. "This, I expected. You are a man much like myself."

Damian was coming to the conclusion that might not be a good thing where his future wife was concerned.

Lia sipped her champagne, feeling numb as the noise of the wedding reception ebbed and flowed around her. She'd married again. Even knowing her reasons for doing so, she was having a hard time accepting that she had stood before a priest and five hundred guests to recite wedding vows two hours before.

She was now Rosalia Marquez…for a while anyway. Damian's years living in America showed themselves in different ways. His desire for her to take his last name was one of them.

His hand against her waist burned into her like a brand. It spoke of possession and feelings she had not anticipated plagued her.

She had thought that knowing he was a blackmailing bastard like her grandfather would have inured her to feelings of guilt, but she'd been wrong. It was so obviously apparent that he was pleased with their marriage, she hated thinking what her revelations later would mean to him.

He would be embarrassed, maybe not as much as if she was the one who did the walking out, but it would still be a source of public speculation. While she did not care what the dozens of people filling the luxury hotel's ballroom thought, she got the impression he did.

He had kept her by his side almost constantly since the wedding ceremony and already several people had commented teasingly on his besotted behavior. She knew he wasn't besotted. He was keeping a close eye on his newest acquisition and that knowledge should diminish her guilt as well.

It didn't. She wasn't like her grandfather and Damian. She had a very difficult time being ruthless when she needed to be and if it weren't for Kaylee's illness, she would never have had the temerity to embark on her current plan.

It would have been so much easier if he'd done as she expected. He had not used the reception as an opportunity to cement business contacts in a social setting and he had vetoed her grandfather's suggestion that Kaylee be excluded from the reception. Lia had learned that from her mother.

Damian had made it clear he wanted children to attend with their parents and for Kaylee to feel welcome. Lia's daughter was already half in-love with the man she believed was to be her father from now on.

Lia had hoped to avoid that kind of bonding by staying in the States until the last minute, but Kaylee and Damian had grown very close, very fast. It had only been a small step apparently for the little girl to make the transition in her mind from new friend to stepfather for Damian. She was already calling him Papa and every time she did, it tore at Lia's heart.

At this point, she might very well have stayed married to him if she could, if only for her daughter's sake.

Only the choice wasn't hers. If it had been, all her high-minded ideals to make Kaylee's life a happy one with her own Papa would probably go flying out the window anyway…the next time Damian showed his ruthless side. There was no telling what a man who would use a child's illness for blackmail was capable of doing, she reminded herself.

Nevertheless, she was glad he had insisted on Kaylee's attendance at the reception. Whatever emotional aftermath Lia would have to face because of it, she was happy to have her daughter nearby. While Kaylee's condition was far from critical, just knowing the little girl had a hole in her heart made Lia feel over-protective and nervous about having Kaylee out of her sight.

She scampered among the guests now, playing a low-key game of tag with several other children under the age of six. They didn't run, but scooted around adult bodies they used as barriers to tag one another. No one seemed to mind and Lia wasn't about to curb the innocent play otherwise.

Seeing her daughter happy was one of the main joys in Lia's life. She often thanked God that while she'd been forced to give up the intimacy of marriage, she had been given the gift of motherhood.

"Señora Marquez?"

Lia turned from watching her daughter to look into the face of her grandfather's extremely efficient accountant. She had learned only that morning, he was also Damian's accountant. Normally he would not have been invited to an occasion of such familial importance, but he had a job to do here today.

"Yes?"

"The funds have been transferred. If you would like to come with me, you can verify the deposit into your account."

She nodded and set her glass of champagne on a table behind her before moving away from Damian.

He grabbed her wrist, stopping midspate in a somewhat heated discussion about the latest Spanish football loss with one of her distant cousins. "Where are you going?"

"To verify the funds transfer."

His mouth tightened in obvious disapproval. "Does that have to happen now?"

Mindful of her cousin's undisguised interest, she merely nodded instead of telling him that if he wanted her to leave the building with him later, it did. "I won't be long."

"When you return, we will make our exit."

"Fine." The sooner she got the big revelations over with the better.

It was weighing more and more heavily on her mind.

"I will tell your mother."

Maria-Amelia planned to keep Kaylee while Damian and Lia went on their honeymoon. Lia had agreed to the two-week separation without argument because she knew it would only actually last one night. Maybe not even a full night.

"Thank you."

When Lia pulled up her online banking page, the uncertainty and fear she had been feeling for the six weeks since learning of her daughter's condition finally began to dissolve. There was enough money in her account to not only cover the surgery, but to pay for all living expenses for the six months following so Lia could stay home full-time with Kaylee. Happy tears washed into her eyes and she had to bite down hard to keep a sob of relief from escaping.

Her baby would be safe now.

No matter what happened in her marriage to Damian, Kaylee would be all right.

The accountant cleared his throat and turned away. She kept staring at the bank balance, unable to look away from the number that represented a new lease on life for her daughter.

"Kaylee is safely with your mother."

Damian.

She didn't want him to see her blubbering like an idiot and she wiped hastily at her tear wet cheeks before turning to face him.

Damian put his hand out, his expression blank but for the fires burning in his dark eyes. "It is time to go."

They were in the back of the long black stretch limo, pulling out of Alicante, before he spoke directly to her again. "We should be at the villa in a little more than an hour."

They were headed north. She wondered if it were near Calpe, or maybe Benidormo. "Is the house yours?"

"Yes. It has singular significance to me." He smiled. "Soon it will be the place of more very special memories."

"What's its significance?"

His eyes laughed at her for the sidestepping, but he answered. "It is the first property I bought after making enough money to do so."

"I thought you lived most of the year in New York."

"I do, but Spain is the land of my birth. I wanted a piece of property to call my own here. I have a caretaker, though, because I only make it over two, or maybe three times a year."

"That must be why we've never met."

He opened the minifridge and pulled out two bottles of sparkling water which he poured into glasses. "You are mistaken."

"I would have remembered meeting you." This man with his glossy black hair and sculpted features was unforgettable.

"You were only a girl at the time, not even eighteen."

Thinking back to that time, when she had been so desperate to get out of her grandfather's house, she realized she could have met King Kong and not noticed. Still, it surprised her she hadn't remembered him. She would never forget him again, no matter how much she might want to.

He was smiling again, watching her with that hungry jaguar expression she'd noticed the first night they met. "Even then, I thought you were beautiful."

She took a sip of the fizzy water he'd handed her.

His expression altered subtly, taking on a truly feral cast. "I wanted you."

She choked. Water sprayed across the seat and onto the pristine white of his tuxedo jacket.

He leaned forward and pounded her back while she tried to breathe again. "Surely this is not such a shock to you?"

She took a trembling breath and then another. "I…" She started wiping at the water with some paper serviettes and her voice faded as she realized she had no idea what she wanted to say.

He took the napkins from her hand and set them aside along with her glass, his gaze hot enough to singe even *her* nerve endings.

She sucked in more air and tried to calm her galloping pulse, but it didn't do any good.

Her gaze was snared by mahogany rich eyes. "You are a beautiful, desirable woman and now you are mine."

She wasn't expecting his next move, or she would have tried to get away, but she landed in his lap in the same moment she realized his intention to put her there. By then it was too late for evasive action.

He cupped her face and that quickly, she was back to the way she'd been on the terrace that night four weeks ago. Immobile in the face of sensations she had never experienced and did not understand.

Once again, she could not make her mouth form the words of protest she knew had to be said. All she could manage was a much too husky, "Damian."

"I have spent twenty-nine nights fantasizing about this moment. I wake remembering the taste of your lips under mine and while I understood your desire to wait, I have not enjoyed the sacrifice. No more sacrifice, Lia," he said as his mouth covered hers with uncompromising passion.

She fell into the kiss like a climber standing on the edge of the cliff with the ground giving way beneath her. No safety rope stopped her freefall to a place she could not see. Her thoughts became a swirling vortex of color and sensation while her lips learned the contours, depth and warmth of Damian's mouth.

Damian tasted the passion and need on Lia's lips and it was all he could do not to strip her and take her right then, but this was their wedding night and he would make it one for his bride to remember.

She felt so perfect in his arms. She fit him exactly, her breasts pressed against his chest, her bottom caressing his sex with little wiggles she doubted she was even aware of. She didn't seem to be aware of anything but his lips and he liked that—more than he would have thought possible.

This woman who had just become his wife was truly his.

His woman. His wife. His family.

He curled his hand around her rib cage, loving the soft feminine curve of her under the silk jacket she wore. He caressed her, brushing his thumb up to tease the underswell of her breast and then down again to press against her hipbone in a statement of sexual possession.

There were many spots on a woman's body only her lover would touch, only a few of which most women, or men for that matter, ever gave serious thought to. A woman's hipbone, the inside of her thigh, behind her knee, the portion of her rib cage just below her breast, her tailbone, the indentation of her waist—they were all spots on Lia that now belonged to Damian and no other man would touch them again.

He laid claim to each one with contact he knew would arouse, concentrating on drawing forth her pleasure bit by bit until she was panting and squirming in a mindless frenzy of passion on his lap. The touching had impacted them both and his erection was so hard, it ached and jumped with every movement of her perfectly shaped derriere.

He broke his mouth from hers and she made a mewing sound that turned his need up one more notch. "It is all right, *querida*. I will give you what you want, but first I must taste your soft skin."

She stared up at him, her amber eyes dazed in a face flushed with desire. "T-taste me?"

"*Sí.*" Did she think he meant that he would put his mouth on the essence of her here in the back of the limousine and did the idea offend her?

It excited him, but was not what he had meant. He

showed her what he wanted, sipping at the smooth skin of her neck and laving the hollow of her collarbone before lifting her hand to suckle at the pulsepoint on her wrist.

She moaned and her head dropped back against his shoulder as if she had not the strength to keep it up one second longer.

"You are sweet and just a tiny bit salty, *mi mujer.*"

"Damian, oh, please…"

He kissed her palm with his teeth and tongue while he peeled her jacket off. She let him do whatever he wanted and her trusting abandon drove his need to please her to a fever pitch.

He sucked her thumb into his mouth and she arched against him. Biting the pad he began to unbutton her blouse. He loosened one slow button at a time, the whole time sucking on one small, feminine finger after another. He was on her final pinky when the last button came undone and the sheer blouse parted to reveal the perfection of her skin beneath. Her bra fastened in the front and he undid it with one deft flick of his fingers. Firm, tip tilted, generous curves spilled out of their restraints and he twitched in his trousers, a small convulsion wetting the tip of his sex.

"Exquisito," he said on a sigh as raspberries and cream perfection filled his vision.

He dipped his head and tasted the valley between her breasts, knowing that the brush of his hair against her sensitive skin would excite her and the way he avoided her tender points would drive her mad.

He was right. She grabbed his head, her own thrashing from side to side against his shoulder. "Damian, what are you doing to me?"

He would have laughed if he wasn't so busy trying not to climax right then and there.

He kissed his way up her chest, to the graceful column of her throat and finally to her lips. They were parted on a moan and he penetrated her mouth with a deep, possessive thrust of his tongue. She stiffened against him and pressed her ripe curves against the wall of his chest while sucking on his tongue as if he offered her the ambrosia of the gods.

He played with her breasts, kneading them, caressing them lightly and then more firmly, but always avoiding the nipples now puckered to pebble-hard points. She moved against him as if she didn't know how to get what she needed.

CHAPTER FOUR

DAMIAN had never made love to a virgin, but if he had, he was sure this is what it would have been like.

Lia had been married three years, but she started at every new pleasure. She moaned like a woman possessed from an admittedly carnal kiss, but only a kiss nonetheless, and squirmed against his sex as if she had no idea what effect her movements were having on him.

She might not know what it was she wanted—though he found that difficult to believe, but he had no doubts about it. He once again broke the lock of their lips to lower his head and take one rosy ripe nipple into his mouth. He started suckling and she screamed. It was the sound of a woman shocked by pleasure, in thrall with her own pleasure and aching for more. He gave it to her. She called his name, then screamed again and started thrusting her hips in an ancient gesture of wanton invitation.

He took the invitation, sliding his hand up the inside of her thigh and then cupping her mound in another moment of possession so primitive he could barely admit it to himself.

She came apart in his arms with a long, keening moan and quivering convulsions that shook her body with their force. He gently rubbed her through the thin silk of her panties and seconds later, she came again, this time bowing toward his hand, her hips lifting off his lap.

He would have consummated their marriage right then if she had not started sobbing in great agonizing shudders. Her reaction so surprised him that he went completely still.

"Oh, Damian…" She said his name over and over again while tears streamed down her face and her body curled into his in a defensive posture he could not mistake.

She was shattered by her reaction and totally incapable of coping with it.

"Shh…*querida*. You must not cry. It is all right." He said other such things, not knowing if they were the right things. He had very little experience with weeping women and her tears unmanned him as a room full of executive sharks did not.

Damian's calming words and soothing caresses finally penetrated the emotional cataclysm roaring through Lia. Her crying diminished to a few hiccuping sobs and she took the snowy-white handkerchief he offered and mopped herself up.

She couldn't look at him, though. She didn't know what had happened. One second she was going to tell him to stop and the next her body was on a journey it had never taken, one more exhilarating than the fastest roller coaster ride in the world and more terrifying as well.

Silence had reigned for several minutes when he tilted her head back and looked into her eyes, his own dark with concern. "Are you all right, *mi esposa bonita?*"

His beautiful wife? Tears washed into her eyes again and she choked on the yes she was trying to get out. She wasn't his wife, not really and never could be.

"You must tell me what is wrong. Are you upset I touched you so freely in the car? The privacy window is shut. No one knows of our intimacy."

Intimacy. She had never known it. Not like this. And after she told him her truth, she would never know it again.

"I'm not worried about that," she forced herself to say.

"Then what has upset you so much?"

She pulled the edges of her shirt together in a defensive gesture not lost on him and his expression plainly told her so. It also questioned her sanity. He wasn't alone in that. She was wondering about her mental stamina right now herself.

"I don't understand what just happened to me," she admitted.

He stared at her as if she had spoken a language he did not understand, not English, which he was as fluent in as his native Spanish.

"I went crazy," she tried to explain. Maybe he was used to kissing women and causing that sort of reaction, but she'd never had it before. "My body, it… Well, I felt things. Amazing things… Like everything inside me contracted and exploded at once. It's frightening."

So was the look of fascinated disbelief on his face. "You climaxed."

No, that was impossible. "You weren't inside me."

"You only climaxed with your husband inside you before?"

She almost laughed at the ridiculous question, but was afraid if she started, she wouldn't stop. "No."

"Then…"

"I never…um…did that at all." She could hardly accept she'd done so now in a car on the road to her new husband's villa.

Did nice girls do that? She'd be afraid she was a closet sex maniac if she didn't know the vicious truth.

Still, this was incredibly embarrassing. Her mother's idea of a sex talk had been to suggest Lia read a few of the racier romance novels. She *had* read a couple before getting married, but her experience with Toby had been so different than the one the authors wrote about that she had never picked up another. Reading about whole women capable of responding sexually only made her feel like more of a failure.

"You have never climaxed?" Damian asked with obvious shock and absolutely no tact.

She felt heat pouring into her face like someone had turned on an oven inside her head. "No."

"You mean with a man, right?" At that moment, he sounded much more American than Spanish and she almost wished he had a little of her grandfather's fixation with polite behavior.

Grandfather would die before asking a woman if she'd engaged in self-pleasuring.

"No."

"Not at all?"

"Stop sounding so shocked. Some women don't you know."

"You were married for three years."

"So?"

He shook his head, his expression dazed. "I have a feeling being married to me is going to be very different for you."

No kidding.

"And there is nothing to be ashamed about if you've given yourself pleasure before."

If the floor of the car opened up right then and she disappeared through it, she would thank God six times a day and seven on Sundays. "Can we not talk about this please?"

"We are married."

"I'm aware of that."

"There should be no secrets between us in this regard."

Where did he get his marital advice? A tacky talk show? Of course women kept secrets. "Some things are private."

"But—"

"I've never done that, all right?" she said with total exasperation and then wanted to hide her face in her hands.

How could he have pushed her so far she'd blurted something that private out loud?

"You've been a widow longer than you were married."

More than three years. "I know that."

"I suppose your mother told you it was wrong?"

"No, I just never wanted to." She had learned to almost hate her femininity. No way was she going to try touching herself to bring pleasure. Besides, being touched down there hurt, or at least it had before.

Damian's hand against her most secret flesh had brought indescribable pleasure. She'd barely even noticed when her vaginal walls started spasming in the contractions that would prevent intercourse. For once her body's inadequacy simply hadn't mattered.

A long drawn out yawn surprised her and she hastily covered her mouth with her hand.

"You are tired now."

"Is that normal?"

"*Sí*. You are sated and your body therefore is ready to relax into sleep."

"Doesn't seem fair to you," she mumbled as she let him press her head against his chest, more than ready to abandon the embarrassing conversation.

"I will have my pleasure later."

He wouldn't, but wild horses would not have dragged that confession out of her at that moment. She was too busy wallowing in the aftermath of the only truly pleasurable intimacy she had ever known.

Lia woke to the sensation of being carried. She savored the feel of Damian's warm, strong arms around her, knowing it would be the last time and wishing it could be different.

She let her eyes slide open and saw that he was carrying her up a flight of stairs. The villa was bathed in late-afternoon light, the peach colored walls warm with the burnished glow from the sun. The staircase was stone with a wrought-iron balustrade and his shoes made a clicking sound on each stair.

"Where are you taking me?" she asked in a still drowsy whisper.

"To bed."

That woke her up fast and she tried to sit up in his arms. "We can't!"

"I assure you, we can."

"Damian, there is something I have to tell you."

"It can wait, but I cannot, *querida.*"

"You have to. Please, let me tell you."

They were in a large bedroom at the front of the house now and he set her carefully down on the bed. "Speak, but be quick. I have little patience left."

Her gaze dropped to the front of his tuxedo trousers and she gulped down air. He wasn't kidding. If this was his normal state of arousal, she doubted they would have fit even if she didn't have her problem.

"I…"

He looked at her expectantly, waiting for her to continue.

She had spent the last four weeks relishing the thought of telling Damian Marquez how her body would thwart both him and her grandfather's wishes.

Only now that the moment of truth had come, the righteous anger that had fueled her since agreeing to her grandfather's blackmail had deserted her. Several emotions fought for supremacy in her battered heart, but not one of them was satisfaction at outwitting the two blackmailing men.

She had hated her inadequacy too long to be sanguine about revealing it, even to thwart the despicable attempt at blackmail.

Though she had vowed never to put herself in such a circumstance again, once more, she felt like a failure as a woman. "You cannot make love to me, Damian."

He looked down at himself and then back at her

where she lay on the bed, her blouse buttoned, but the bra still unfastened and her nipples showing through. "Are you sure about that?"

"I'm positive." Tears clogged her throat and she had to swallow twice before continuing. "We can't. You have to believe me."

His eyes registered comprehension. "Is it that time of month?"

She wished she could take the easy out, but a face-saving lie would only put off for later what was better faced now.

"No."

"Then what is the problem?"

"I've never had another lover besides my husband. I mean, I haven't even dated since Toby's death."

"Your grandfather told me this."

"I bet he didn't tell you that you were the first man I've even kissed in more than three years."

His brows drew together. "I do not understand the problem here. To be truthful, knowing the only other man who has shared your body is no longer in this world satisfies the throwback in me."

"There's a reason I stayed away from other men."

"You were mourning your husband. Your grandfather told me. Do you still love him? Is that the problem?" He didn't sound nearly so complacent now. In fact, extremely irritated would be a much better description. "You feel you are betraying him by taking me to your bed?"

The compassionate question asked with such obvious male impatience made her want to smile, but the truth made her want to cry even more. "No. I *can't* take any man to my bed. I can't make love, Damian. My body won't let me. I freeze up." Which was not the whole truth, but enough of it for him to get the picture.

"You were raped?" he asked, looking ready to kill someone.

"What?"

"You speak as if you have been traumatized in a sexual way. You say your body will not allow you to make love, that you freeze up. These are classic reactions for a woman who has been hurt sexually."

Did she have to tell him everything? Wasn't it bad enough that her body had let her down in this way for so long? Why did she have to humiliate herself by spelling her flaw out to him? "I was never raped."

His eyes said he didn't believe her.

"I wasn't. I promise, Damian. That is not the problem."

"Then what is? You are too passionate to live like a nun, Lia."

That made her laugh, though the sound was not a pleasant one. Passionate? Not likely. "I'm about as sexual as an amoeba."

"You are kidding, right?"

She just stared at him.

"You responded to me both that night on the terrace and on the way here. You are not sexless. You came twice today with little more touching than what is usual for foreplay."

Really? *That was foreplay?* Not like any she'd ever experienced before. "But that's *all* I can do, Damian. The truth is, I didn't even know I could do that much."

And she wouldn't have been able to if she wasn't

feeling something more for him than mere physical attraction, she was sure of it. Her emotions hit overload on that admission. It was the final blow to defenses sieged for weeks on end.

How many nights had she lain awake wondering how she would pay for Kaylee's surgery and if surgery was even the right choice for her daughter? She'd come to Spain with the intention of swallowing her pride and asking her grandfather for money. But her pride had taken a lot more abasement than a family size serving of humble pie. She had been blackmailed into bartering her body in marriage to the first man she'd responded to sexually since shortly after her disastrous wedding night.

Realizing that she might actually be starting to care for him on an emotional level, no matter how shallow, took what was left of her peace of mind and destroyed it.

Her body started shaking with reaction, like she was in shock and if she didn't concentrate very hard, she was going to hyperventilate. Weak tears she hated because they revealed a vulnerability she didn't want exposed rushed into her eyes and tightened her throat.

As they spilled over, she surged to her feet. "P-please believe me, Damian. I c-can't make l-love with you." She was shaking so badly, she was stuttering. "Let me sleep somewhere else. I c-can't...I can't share that bed with you."

She stumbled past him, but he reached out as if to stop her and she reeled backward, bumping into the wall. "P-please... Don't touch me!"

"I will not allow you to go off on your own in this state." He moved inexorably forward and swung her into his arms before she could argue further. "You will sleep here. I will find another bed if you insist, but first you must calm down."

"I can't. I can't handle it any m-more. *Not any of it.*" She sobbed into his shirtfront, not bothering to question how she could find comfort in the arms of the enemy.

He sat down with her on the end of the bed and held her while she cried for the second time that day, but this time it was grief not gratitude and shock that sent her emotions careening out of control. He soothed her, much as he would a child and she let him, her tears finally subsiding after she'd thoroughly soaked his shirt.

She pressed against his chest and he allowed her to move off his lap.

He stood up, his expression grim. "Get into your nightgown. I will be back shortly."

Then he was gone. She didn't know where and didn't really care. She only wished he wasn't coming back. She felt like such an idiot crying all over him. She was certainly giving him some kind of a wedding night. From her response in the car, he had to have been looking forward to making love and she'd shut him down and then lost her emotional control all over him.

Even blackmailers deserved better treatment.

Realizing she didn't know how long he would be gone and terrified he might return while she was still undressing, she started fumbling the buttons open on her shirt. She ended up ripping the blouse trying to get it off, but by the time she'd stripped, she was sufficiently composed to contemplate a shower. Hot water and the privacy of a shower stall seemed incredibly alluring in that moment.

When she came out, Damian sat on a chair beside the bed, his tie and jacket gone. His shirt was unbuttoned several buttons, revealing a slice of bronzed chest lightly covered in black curling hair. While his clothes and posture were relaxed, his expression was forbidding.

She swallowed a sigh and tamped down the urge to turn around and spend the rest of the night hiding in the bathroom. "I'm sorry."

"Tomorrow we will talk, when you have rested. For now, I want you to drink this." He held up a brandy snifter half-filled with the dark amber liquid.

She wasn't particularly fond of the stuff, but she did not demur. It had been a tumultuous day and her insides felt shredded.

She took the glass and sipped at it.

"Are you afraid of me?" He lounged back in the chair, his feet crossed at the ankles and she realized they were bare.

"No."

"You are my wife. You belong to me."

"Yes." At least she agreed with the wife part, she wasn't so sure about belonging to him, but she'd had enough confrontation for one day.

"I would like to sleep with you in my arms tonight."

All the tension that the hot water from the shower had drained out of her came back. "I can't…"

"Make love. *Sí.* You have made this patently clear, but you can allow your husband to hold you, can you not?"

"Toby moved to another bed three months after Kaylee was born. He said it was too hard to sleep next to me and not be able to make love to me."

"I am not your former husband. If I make a request, be assured I know the limitations of what I ask. I think that tonight, you do not need to be alone."

The offer was such a generous one, after what she had told him that she didn't know what to say.

"Say you will allow me to hold you through the night," he said, letting her know she'd voiced her disconcertion aloud.

"Yes." It was selfish of her, but she hadn't been held in such a long time, and tonight he was right…the last thing she wanted was to be left with the loneliness her failures had forced on her.

She finished her brandy and climbed into the bed. Damian removed his clothes down to his boxers and then joined her, pulling her into his arms and curving his body around hers. She felt cosseted and protected.

"Thank you," she whispered as he pressed a button above the headboard that cut the lights.

"It is both my right and my pleasure. Be assured this is where I meant to be this night."

She could feel the resurgence of his arousal and doubted his words, knowing he would get nothing but frustration from sleeping with her. However, he did not complain and she had to wonder if his assertion of rights indicated his male pride was involved in some way.

Too weary to think about it, she allowed the steady beat of his heart to lull her into a dreamless sleep that lasted until morning.

She woke alone, but the smell of coffee alerted her that Damian was close by. She turned over and found him in the chair he had occupied the night before. A mug of steaming coffee rested in one hand while the newspaper rustled in the other.

She scooted into a sitting position, letting the covers slip to her waist. Her cotton pajamas were anything but revealing.

"Good morning."

The newspaper came down and chocolate-dark eyes gave her a serious appraisal. "Good morning. You slept well."

It was not a question, but she answered it anyway. "Yes, thank you. Did you?" she asked, not without some trepidation.

"After I reasoned many things out, I slept." He laid the paper and his cup of coffee aside. Then he picked up a carafe she had not noticed before. "Would you like some?"

"Yes, please."

He poured it, his expression meditative. "You did not intend our marriage to last, did you?"

"No." There was no point in prevaricating; besides he was smart enough to know the truth. "I did not believe you would want to stay married once you knew the truth."

He nodded and handed the cup to her, nothing of his reaction to her words revealed in his face. However, his demeanor was every bit as forbidding as it had been the night before.

She took a sip, savoring the rich chicory taste while wishing life could be even half so pleasant. "I'm sorry. I realize now that no matter how angry I was with you and my grandfather, what I have done is just as wrong."

"Marrying me with no intention of keeping your promise?" he asked.

"I didn't intend to break my promise."

That seemed to interest him and he studied her in silence for several seconds. "You thought that I would back out of the marriage and you would therefore have kept your end of the bargain. Your sense of integrity would remain inviolate?"

"Yes." But she'd been wrong. She felt like a cheat even if she had been forced into her circumstances.

"You did not consider refusing to make love to me an action that would undermine our marriage?"

"It isn't something I have a choice about."

"You are sure of this?"

"Yes."

"How? If you have had no intimate relationships since the death of your husband?"

"It didn't work with him, either."

Damian tensed. "Did he hurt you?"

"Not intentionally."

"But unintentionally?"

"Yes, just as I unintentionally hurt him."

Damian weighed her words while she finished her coffee. "Explain why you believed I deserved to be married under false pretenses."

He was so calm, she could hardly believe it. Any other man would be yelling by now, but Damian acted like he was on a fact-finding mission for a new business venture.

She wasn't so sanguine. Just thinking about what he and her grandfather had done to her, the pain and fear they had put her through made her see red. "Only a monster would use the life of a child to blackmail a woman into marriage."

That startled him and his dark eyes narrowed. "Explain."

"Don't feign ignorance."

"And yet, I sit here before you…ignorant. Do you wish me to call Benedicto and ask him? I assume he knows the details of this *blackmail*."

Not wanting her grandfather brought into this, Lia explained, even though Damian had to know already. She played his distorted game, but let him know in every way possible what she thought of the threats used to coerce her.

When she was done, he stood up and walked to the window. It overlooked the ocean, but she doubted the view of the beautiful waters of the Costa Blanca was what drew him there at the moment. In point of fact, it was the place in the room farthest from her and she felt his withdrawal as if it were a physical line being reeled in, pulling all his life energy away from her.

"Did it never occur to you that I might be unaware of Benedicto's methods of persuasion?"

"No. How could Grandfather believe he could get away with it otherwise? I was under no obligation to keep it from you."

"And yet you did."

"Only because I knew you knew." That hadn't made a lot of sense, but he didn't ask her to clarify.

"Did I? Your grandfather is a master tactician and he outmaneuvered both of us."

"No." A sick feeling started growing in the pit of her stomach and she put her almost empty cup down, knowing she would be unable to drink any more. "What do you mean?"

"I believed you married me because you wanted to assure your future and that of your daughter, perhaps even to please your grandfather. I was unaware Kaylee faced such a serious health complication."

"And if you had been?"

He turned back toward her, but stayed by the window. "I am not sure it would have changed the outcome, but I would have better understood your reaction to me yesterday."

"Grandfather said you are a shrewd businessman and would expect something for the money you gave to me."

"This is true. However, you are not."

"Not what?"

"Shrewd when it comes to business. You should have asked for a great deal more in an up-front settlement. It surprised me that Benedicto did not insist upon it, but I assumed he saw himself in debt to me."

"In debt to you? He said you'd helped him out financially over the past few years." She hadn't really understood what that had meant and hadn't cared beyond the fact Benedicto could not pay for Kaylee's surgery.

"His fortune was severely reduced by poor investments. Not the ones he made in my company, I might add."

"Naturally."

"In order to continue living at his current standard, he sold his villa to me."

"But…"

"The agreement included him living there for his lifetime and me providing a home for your mother upon his death."

"But the villa belongs to you?"

"Yes, among other things. In this way, he was able to maintain many of his business holdings and keep your mother in comfort."

"But—"

"That is unimportant. We have more pressing matters to discuss right now."

"Our marriage."

"And its future." The way he said *future* sent shivers down her spine.

"We don't have a future."

"I disagree." He held up his hand when she opened her mouth to argue. "*Silence.* You took vows before God and many people yesterday, as did I."

"But…" He was right she had, only she hadn't been thinking of them as binding vows, knowing as she did she could not maintain a true marriage.

His dark eyes narrowed and she thought she would not like to be this man's business adversary. "The question I want answered now is: are you prepared to honor those vows?"

"Why should I be when my daughter's life was used to coerce me into saying them?" she asked with a belligerence that was only surface deep. Underneath she was scared to death.

He caught her gaze with his own and for the first time she saw the emotion he was tamping down. It was pure, unadulterated fury. "And yet, I kept my side of the bargain, did I not?"

In the face of that fury she could only nod dumbly.

"Kaylee can be taken care of now because I will see she is taken care of. Both her and your future are assured so long as you stay as my wife."

"But you want children."

"*Sí.*"

"I can't give them to you."

"That remains to be seen."

"You expect me to try?"

"You owe it to me. It is a promise you made to both myself and your grandfather."

CHAPTER FIVE

BUT it was a promise she had thought she would not have to keep. She let her head fall back against the headboard, her eyes shut tightly against a truth she did not want to acknowledge, but one that refused to be ignored. Her grandfather had ruthlessly manipulated her fear for her daughter to get his way, but she had also ruthlessly used Damian to get the money she needed.

"I'm no better than he is," she whispered.

"You take after him more than he realizes, but I like Benedicto. I do not think this is a bad thing."

Her eyes flew open. "I tricked you into marriage and you don't think that's a bad thing?"

"That depends."

"On what, for Heaven's sake?"

"Whether or not you intend to keep the promises you made and honor the vows you spoke."

She sighed. "I'll keep them," she said dully, "but it won't make any difference. No amount of *trying* will make intimacy possible between us."

She'd learned that with Toby and the prospect of

going through more of the same with Damian made her heart go cold.

"I want you, Lia. I mean to have you."

"But you can't." Wasn't he listening? She hit the bed with both fists. "Don't you understand? *I can't do it.* If I could, I would." And she would if only to maintain her own sense of integrity.

He smiled, all masculine complacency where before fury had reigned. "That is good to know. Now, tell me why you believe you cannot make love to me."

The words fell like stones between them, sending out ripple after ripple of waves through the murky waters surrounding them.

"I don't just *believe* it, I *know* it."

"So tell me why."

"What difference does it make?"

"I want to know."

"Why?" She was going to break apart into itty-bitty pieces if she had to expose her defectiveness to him. "Knowing the cause won't make any difference to the outcome."

"Perhaps, but I believe you owe this explanation to me."

"Apparently you believe I owe you a lot of things."

"Don't you?"

"Maybe." But that didn't make answering any easier. "It hurts to talk about it, can you understand that at least?"

But he wouldn't…couldn't understand. He didn't know what it felt like to be broken and defective.

"I don't want to hurt you," he said.

"But you will if it means learning what you want to know."

"Sometimes you must experience pain before you can get to the pleasure."

"Toby said a similar thing on our wedding night, only the pleasure never came."

"Are you afraid to make love to me because you do not trust me not to physically harm you?"

"Of course not." Though if he tried to make love to her, he wouldn't be able to help hurting her.

"I do not believe it is because you do not want me. You respond too readily and beautifully to my touch."

"I do want you," she admitted with aching honesty, even though right now she would also cheerfully have strangled him.

And she might want him, but no way was she going to care for him. That thought last night had to have been a result of an over stimulated brain.

"Then tell my why you cannot have me." He sounded angry again, and frustrated. She knew that tone. She'd heard it enough in her first marriage.

He said he wanted the truth. She'd give it to him. "I have vaginismus."

He stared back at her with no recognition sparking in his intense, chocolate-brown gaze.

"It's a condition that causes my vaginal muscles to contract involuntarily when I try to make love." She tried to talk about it as clinically as possible, distancing the physical reality of the condition from her, the woman she was inside. "My body will not allow you to penetrate me."

She could not tell if she disappointed him, or disgusted him, or even if he pitied her. "What causes it?"

"I don't know." She had her suspicions. She'd read

a little on the sexual dysfunction, but she didn't really want to know that much about the condition that had robbed her of her femininity.

For six years, the part of a woman's body that was supposed to give her the most pleasure had been Lia's own personal enemy. There had been times during her brief marriage that she hadn't just hated that part of her body, she'd hated herself.

Her doctor had been very clear. He believed the muscular spasms began in her head and she would have to will them to stop. She'd never been able to.

"It happened when you kissed me on the terrace, when you tried to touch me."

Understanding flared in his eyes. "That's why you pulled away from me. I thought you wanted to wait for our wedding night."

He'd thought she wanted to consummate the deal. Right now, she could wish it had been that simple, no matter how cold-blooded.

"At the time I didn't know we were supposed to have a wedding night."

"You thought I expected you to let me make love to you to sweeten a deal for your grandfather." He sounded like he'd just worked that out.

She shrugged. "Frankly I preferred the righteous indignation angle over having to tell you the truth."

"You had this problem with your first husband?"

"Yes. My marriage ended the night he died, but not *from* his death like everyone thinks. He told me he was leaving me and then got in the car and was hit by a drunk driver on his way to a hotel. Toby needed sex like other men, but unlike other women, I couldn't give it to him."

"Lia…" Pity shimmered in the brown depths of Damian's eyes and she wanted to scream.

Toby had looked at her just that way when he asked for the divorce. Seeing it in Damian's expression made her furious.

"Are you satisfied now?" She felt wild with grief and frustration.

Damian winced at the volume of her voice, or was it the look in her eyes?

Unexpectedly he moved and reached toward her, but she jerked away. "Don't! I don't need or want your pity, Damian."

It devastated her to have to reveal her shattered sexuality to him and she wondered how she'd ever thought she could be complacent about it.

"Lia, I did not mean to hurt you, but for us to face the future together, I have to know the facts."

"We don't have a future, or haven't you figured that out yet? All the pity in the world can't change that." She surged off the bed and spun away. "I'm going to take a shower."

She didn't hear him move, but all of a sudden two hands clamped down on her shoulders and spun her around. She didn't even have time to yell at him again before his mouth came down on hers.

It should have been a kiss full of aggression.

His body was fairly vibrating with it, but his lips were gentle and coaxing. She remained stiff against him for as long as she could, but he was offering comfort when she desperately needed comfort and human connection when she was grieving that lack in her life.

Her mouth softened under his lips.

He rubbed his hands up and down her back, soothing her, gentling her. His tongue tasted her, sharing the ambrosia of his mouth with her, but without overt sexual implications.

It was as if he was using his kiss to appease her emotional pain. Then he pulled her melting body into his and she felt the press of his erection against her. Proof that he wanted her, but she could not give him what he wanted and no amount of tears or pain could change that.

Tears nevertheless seeped out of her eyelids and she turned her face away, pushing against him until he let her go.

"I need to get dressed."

"Yes. And then we will talk."

"Haven't we talked enough?"

"No, but it is best left for the moment." He propelled her away from him, a possessive hand caressing her backside. "Go. Take your shower."

Damian wanted to curse in six languages.

He had blackmailed her into marriage. Perhaps he had not known at the time what his money was going for, but the results were the same. She had been forced and his money had been the weapon.

A less hardened man might let her go but he had no intention of taking that route. He wanted her, more than he had ever wanted another woman. He would have her. Somehow. Some way. Damian Marquez did not give up and he had learned how to get the things he wanted in life.

More to the point, Lia was now his wife and that made her his responsibility. She needed someone to rely on, someone on her side, helping her to fight her battles and those of Kaylee.

He had every intention of being that someone.

He would take care of her.

He let out a low curse as he thought of the first husband who had done such a poor job of that very thing.

What kind of man divorced a woman he supposedly loved because she could not give him sex? Not a man…Tobias Kennedy had been an eighteen-year-old boy when he married Lia and not much older when he asked for the divorce. A teenager wouldn't know how to handle the kind of difficulty they'd faced in the marriage bed.

Infierno, the boy had probably thought it was his fault and been too devastated to say so. He had finally given up on trying to make it better and ripped Lia's sexual identity to shreds in the process.

However, Damian was not an inexperienced child with sexual stars in his eyes. He did not believe there was nothing that could be done. There had to be treatment for, what had she called it? *Vaginismus.*

Maybe there was no treatment. He would find out, but even if he could not penetrate her, there were other ways of making love. Ways his body ached to try. He had spent four weeks in a constant state of sexual anticipation and no other woman could relieve his need.

He did not let that bother him. She was his wife. It was only right he wanted her alone. It certainly didn't mean he had feelings for her that could make him vulnerable.

Perhaps their lovemaking could not result in the children he craved, but the potential for pleasure between the two of them was limitless. Did she not realize that?

He suspected she did not. After the experience in the limo the day before, he could conclude only that she knew less about her own sexuality than most teenagers. And this should not surprise him. He knew Maria-Amelia and Benedicto very well. They would not have spoken openly about sexual matters to Lia.

She would have expected Tobias Kennedy to know something, but clearly the young man had not and Lia's perception of herself as a woman had been damaged in the process. Was it really such a surprise that in the three years since the man's death she had ignored the passionate side of her nature completely?

Which left Damian with one burning question.

How soon could he give her another lesson in the pleasure her body was capable of?

Lia found Damian on the upper terrace that overlooked both his private pool and the bright blue sea beyond. The villa was on the side of one of the many hills that lined the Costa Blanca. Surrounded by trees and rock cliffs, it had more privacy than many of the houses she had seen along the way.

She was grateful for that solitude. After their discussion that morning, it would have been torment to be surrounded by other people.

He stood and pulled a chair out for her. "Feeling better?"

Did one feel better after an emotional holocaust? "I'm in control of myself, if that's what is worrying you." She wasn't about to start shouting at him or crying again.

"You are my wife. I am concerned for your emotional well-being. Is that such a shock?"

She determinedly buttered a slice of toast, refusing to let his words instill hope in a heart that had long ago learned the cost of that emotion. "How long do you want me to remain your wife?"

More than likely, for his pride's sake, he would prefer to wait to reveal their separated status for a year, or so.

He poured her a glass of juice. "I recall making life-long vows yesterday and you assured me of your plans to honor those vows earlier this morning."

"And then you learned that I cannot be the wife you need."

"Look at me, Lia."

She'd avoided doing so since sitting down. As her gaze clashed with his, she felt the world around her distort with a sense of unreality. He did not look condemning, or angry, or disappointed, or even pitying.

His expression was filled with masculine stubbornness. She ought to know, she'd seen it often enough on her grandfather's face.

"You told me you would keep your promises."

"You can't want me to."

"You are wrong. In fact, I demand it."

"But it's impossible."

He relaxed back in the oversize wrought-iron outdoor chair. "Climbing a mountain seems impossible until taken one step at a time."

She didn't buy the old-wise-man attitude one bit. This man got what he wanted and right now he wanted value for his money. She couldn't give it to him in the heirs he expected to have from her. What else did he think he could get out of marriage to her?

An awful, heart destroying thought formed. "Do you think I'll make an *understanding* wife? That I will turn a blind eye to you getting from another woman what I can't give you?"

"Would you?"

"No."

"Que bueno. I would not ask you to. I would not be flattered by a wife who does not care if he visits another woman's bed. Now, eat your breakfast before we continue this discussion. You did not take enough sustenance yesterday."

"Has anyone ever mentioned your domineering side to you before?"

"I am a self-made multimillionaire. It is no shocking revelation. Now eat."

She harrumphed, but did as he suggested simply because he was right. She hadn't eaten enough yesterday and she was hungry.

When she was done eating, he called for a woman to take the food away. Lia learned the woman's name was Juana and she was the wife to the man who watched over the property while Damian was away. They acted as housekeeper and gardener/maintenance man while he was in residence.

He stood and put his hand out. "Come, we will hike down to the beach."

Exercise sounded good and she was dressed for it in a pair of casual jeans, T-shirt and tennis shoes. "Let me get my jacket." The spring air was chillier than usual for this time of year.

He was waiting for her outside, his own arms bare in short sleeves and his long legs encased in a pair of black jeans. He had a black backpack slung over one shoulder. "Ready to go?"

She nodded and followed him onto the rocky trail to the beach. He put his hand out to steady her in several places and each time it happened, her body shivered with feelings that had nothing to do with the salt-laden wind blowing her hair around her face.

His nearness impacted her more every time they were together. She'd never felt this way, not in her marriage, not since. It was as if her body was a piano and his nearness pressed keys that resulted in a sonata played along every nerve ending she possessed.

When they reached the beach, the sudden stoppage of the wind surprised her and she looked around. They were in an alcove in the rock face of the cliff she hadn't been able to see from the top of the path. A private paradise of white sand, palm trees and beautiful jagged cliffs surrounded them. There was even a small inlet of water that looked deep enough to swim in near the alcove's opening. The break in the rock face afforded a narrow view of the blue sea, but no one on the beach outside would realize she and Damian were there.

He pulled a brightly colored throw blanket from the backpack and laid it out. "Sit down."

She did, ready for a rest after their trek down the trail. It hadn't been all that tiring, but keeping control of rampaging hormones was another story altogether.

Enjoying the warmth the protected spot afforded, she pulled off her jacket and tossed it aside, then stretched her legs out in front of her. She crossed them at the ankles before leaning back on her elbows and turning her face up to the sun. "It's nice here."

"I like it, but I must admit the beauty today is even more eye-catching than usual." There was an odd note in his voice.

She opened her eyes to see why and found his gaze riveted to the way her posture thrust her full breasts into prominence.

She quickly sat up and crossed her arms over her drawn up knees. "Uh, it's very private."

"Yes." He sat beside her, his dark gaze probing. "Does it bother you that I look at you? You are my wife. You should expect it."

"Being blackmailed into marriage isn't exactly a recipe for trust and togetherness. Besides, I'm not such a witch that I want to tease you with my body when I can't follow through."

Damian frowned. "Let us get one thing straight between us, *mi esposa,* before I lose all patience with you."

"What?"

"You married me to provide a way to take care of Kaylee. It was not a matter of blackmail, but necessity."

"I wouldn't have married you otherwise."

"Perhaps."

"You're too arrogant to be believed."

"No, merely aware of how strongly attracted we are to each other. Ignoring the attraction would have been the challenge, not giving into it."

"I wouldn't have given into it. I knew it couldn't go anywhere."

"You gave a very convincing performance to the contrary on the terrace a month ago and then in the car yesterday."

She was floundering like a fish out of water trying to think of a proper set down, when he asked, "Did your first husband accuse you of teasing him?"

"Sometimes." Even talk of her disastrous marriage was a welcome change of topic from her weakness in controlling her response to Damian. "We were young. He wanted things I couldn't give him. It was hard on us both."

"It is as I thought. You were both too young to handle the challenges your body faced."

"I can't make love, Damian. Age isn't going to change that and as mature and worldly as you might be, you'll quickly grow tired of a wife who can't give you what you want."

"Penetration is not the only form of lovemaking that can give pleasure."

Blood rushed into her cheeks. "You're so blunt."

"What use is there in attempting subtlety when bluntness is what is needed?"

"We don't have to discuss things in their nitty-grittiest detail to know a lifetime commitment between the two of us won't work."

"I do not agree. It is the detail that interests me and will dictate what level of intimacy we can enjoy in our marriage."

"I told you…none."

"Are you saying you cannot bear any touch at all?"

She sighed and then huffed out a frustrated, "No."

"Then intimacy of one form or another is possible, but perhaps you are not aware of this."

"I am aware of it. I'm not stupid."

A small smiled curved his lips. "Not stupid, but naïve, I think."

"I'm not."

He shook his head. "Your innocence showed itself startlingly well in the limousine yesterday."

She felt oh yet another blush coming on and grimaced. Her hot cheeks would be taken as proof of his assertions about her naïveté. And what was the point in pretending otherwise? She was more awkward than a virgin raised by nuns when it came to talking about sex.

"Well, I'm not *that* innocent anyway," she muttered.

"Ah, so you are aware of the many ways a body can give and receive pleasure?" he asked, his eyes mocking.

"Uh, yeah…of course. Who isn't?"

Speaking of bodies, his was awfully close and it was wreaking havoc on her nervous system again. Although she'd never been into self-torment, she couldn't make herself move away from his disturbing nearness.

"And still you think we can have *no* intimacy at all?" His tone questioned her veracity, or her sanity, she wasn't sure which and maybe neither was he.

"It didn't work for me and Toby," she blurted out, frustrated by the growing desire she could do nothing about and the fact he was forcing her to reveal her every failure in the femininity stakes. "Neither of us liked it."

They'd both been extremely embarrassed by the whole thing, even when she tried touching him with the lights off. Using her mouth had been even worse. She just couldn't relax. Nothing fit right and it made her gag, which had really irritated Toby. Needless to say, she'd had very little success giving him any kind of sexual release.

Which had been really demoralizing. Not only had she been incapable of opening her body to her husband, she had not been able to give him pleasure in other ways, either.

"You tried what exactly?"

He wanted her to be blunt, so she'd be blunt. "Touching him with my hand and mouth." Saying it intensified the heat in her face until she felt hot enough to fry an egg, but she forced herself to meet his eyes. "You think I can give you something that will make up for my lack, but *I know* that whatever I can do won't be enough."

"You are wrong." She watched the sensual lips that had given her so much pleasure the day before form the words and wished with everything in her that he was right.

But he wasn't. "No, I'm not. I know, Damian."

He shook his head, his expression rueful. "*Querida,* if you stroked *me* with your hand, it would be *enough.*" It was his turn to shudder, but the sensual cast to his features said it had not been in revulsion. "The mere *idea* of your small, pink tongue touching me *anywhere* on my body excites me to the point of pain."

"But, Toby—"

"Was an eighteen-year-old boy who did not know some very basic things about sex or he would have found a way for both of you to be satisfied. I think also that he was not confident enough to allow you to pleasure him. I have no such inhibitions."

She could imagine. The man didn't have any reticence in what he talked about, he was probably totally abandoned when it came to making love. Maybe it *could* be better with him, but it couldn't be complete and that still posed a problem.

"Toby wasn't the one with a defective body. I was... am. You want children. It was part of our bargain. I can't give them to you."

"That is a matter we will leave for a later date. Let us deal with one issue at a time."

"It's the same issue."

"No, it is not."

She wanted to scream at his deliberate obtuseness.

His eyes told her he knew how frustrated she was, but he wasn't backing down. "Neither you nor Tobias Kennedy had enough experience or maturity to make sex work between you. That will not be a problem between us."

"My body doesn't work! There's no way around that, no matter how *experienced* you are."

"It is not merely a matter of experience. It is also a matter of desire. I want you, Lia, any way I can get you."

"That's what Toby said too, but it wasn't true...not in the long run." Why was he making this so hard for her? Pushing at her until she felt like she would break. Making her think maybe this time things could be different. Hope was an insidious emotion and she'd had her share of it shattered.

It was killing her that he kept trying to make her deficiency sound like it was less of a problem than she knew it to be.

He leaned over her and cupped her nape. His thumb pressed against her chin, gently preventing her from opening her mouth when she tried to say something else. "Your vaginal walls spasm and that prevents intercourse. That does not mean your sexuality is dead or that your entire body does not work."

She jerked her head back so she could talk, even in the midst of her misery wishing she could stay connected to his touch. "You don't understand—"

"Lia, *mi mujer,* you are the one who does not understand." He tilted her chin up until her lips were a breath away from his. "There are infinite ways to make love."

He kissed her, a soft, slow melding of their mouths that sent tremors of awareness skating along unused nerve endings.

"It sounds to me—" another soft, slow kiss "—like you did not try—" a gentle nibble of her lips "—any of them—" he kissed her again, a longer, more evocative kiss "—with much effect."

By the time he lifted his head, she was trembling and could only stare at him, dazed.

"There is a lot you do not know, *mi querida inocente.*"

Remembering her very first orgasm, at his hand, her bemused brain conceded that maybe he was right and the tiniest flicker of hope began to smolder inside her. She'd never experienced anything like it. Perhaps the magician who could make her body do that could find a pleasure in her body she had not believed could be found there.

Still, she had to ask, "What if I don't please you?"

He ran his thumb over her kiss swollen lips. "It is not possible. But let us say for expedient's sake and so you will quit arguing with me—if there is a problem, I will fix it."

"Toby thought he could fix it, too…"

"Tobias Kennedy was the husband of your girlhood,

I am the husband of your womanhood. I can handle it."
Arrogant confidence stared her down and she found
herself believing.

CHAPTER SIX

"ARE you willing to try, Lia?"

"I don't really have a choice, do I? I gave my promise and if I can keep it, I will."

He didn't appear bothered by her bitter words. In fact, he smiled. "You will learn you do not have to hide behind this front of false anger."

He thought her anger was false? God help her if that was true because without it, she would be defenseless.

Before she could answer the ridiculous accusation, he kissed her again, this time letting his lips linger, coaxing hers to response. He cherished her mouth until her tension drained away and she was clinging to him, emotion swamping her in terrifying, but beautiful waves.

He withdrew his lips, his breathing irregular. "I'm shaking with the need to touch you and be touched by you." His big body trembled, giving credence to his words, no matter how hard she found them to believe. "Do not deny me."

She didn't intend to, but old fears rose to haunt her. "What if you want intercourse…after the touching? Toby always did."

The passion gave way to a sulfuric narrow-eyed gaze that went through her like shards of breaking glass. "*Infierno,* I am not a teenager with rampaging hormones. I am a thirty-year-old man who understands the limits you have laid before me. I will not pressure for what you cannot give."

"You've been pressuring me for the past half an hour."

"For what I know you can give and will be glad for doing so. Trust me to know what is best."

His angry demand had the peculiar effect of calming her fears. A man like Damian would not insist she trust him if he did not believe with absolute certainty he could deliver. His pride would not allow him to do anything else.

He took a visible rein on that Spanish temper that had blown up so unexpectedly. "If I say we can make love in a way that will leave us both satisfied, you need to believe me."

The promise in his voice and dark brown gaze went deep inside her, touching a place she'd kept locked tight for years. It left her with no alternative but to ride the wave of desire threatening to drown her.

She took a deep breath and plunged. "You'll have to show me what to do. I don't know how to please you."

Damian shook his head, finding it hard to believe she was so worried about that. Couldn't she see the effect she had on him? He had not been lying when he told her one touch would be enough. If she put her hand on him right now, he would explode.

"This is not about pleasing me," he said, wishing he could bury the words so deep in her mind, she would never again doubt them. "What we do together is about finding pleasure in one another. I guarantee you, we will do so."

Damian watched as one expression after another flitted across her face in response to his words. There was still some uncertainty and as much as he wanted to simply start touching her, she had to be sure this was what she wanted.

"Okay," she said softly.

"Are you certain?" He would have her, but not as the result of rape or coercion. She would come to him willingly, or not at all.

Her golden eyes misty, she nodded. "I trust you, Damian."

Something inside him contracted at that assurance. "I will not allow you to regret placing your trust in me." He cupped her cheek, the skin soft like silk. "You are so beautiful."

"Oh, Damian…"

He had to taste her lips. Really taste them, not just kiss them. He closed the slight distance between their mouths. She parted her lips on a soft sigh and he licked them, tracing the pretty pink contours before slipping his tongue inside her mouth and savoring the sweetness waiting for him there.

Her response was shy at first, but he gently teased her until her sexy little tongue followed his back into his mouth. He sucked on it and she moaned.

He concentrated on kissing her into a state where she would allow him to do whatever he pleased. It would require the lowering of her inhibitions completely for this time of intimacy to succeed in giving them both what they needed.

He pushed her backward and she let him lower her to the blanket, opening her body to him on the first level of sensual intimacy. When she began to move on the blanket, he knew it was time to take the touching to the next level.

He slid his hand down her rib cage and then back up again, this time under the hem of her short T-shirt. Once again, her bra had a front catch and he disposed of it easily without removing his lips from hers. He peeled back the silk and cupped the petal softness of her breast, brushing one thumb over her already straining nipple.

She whimpered against his lips and he knew she was remembering yesterday, like he was, when she'd come so close to climaxing from him merely touching her breasts.

She was so responsive, more than any woman he had ever known. How could she have this condition that prevented her from experiencing the full range of her sensuality?

He squeezed her generous breast, unexpected shivers going through him at the feel of her hard peak against his palm. It was tame loveplay, but it impacted him as he had never been impacted by a woman, no matter how experienced in the art of love.

Small, feminine fingers began exploring him, touching and testing him until he thought he would go mad with it. His own hand moved down to cup her through her jeans. Even the thick denim could not hide the level of her arousal and knowing she was excited heightened his own desires to a fever pitch.

Then he felt a touch as light as butterfly wings against the fly of his jeans and he jerked his mouth from hers, uttering a low growl from deep in his chest.

Her hand stilled, but her eyes glowed dark amber. "Do you like that?"

"Yes," he hissed as she grew bolder, cupping him much the same way he held her.

Her smile about took his breath away. "I want to touch you all over."

"There is nothing I would like more, but first will you grant me a favor?"

"What?" she asked, her breath hitching as his fingers pressed against the seam of her jeans.

"A woman has an infinite capacity for sensual enjoyment, but a man does not recover so quickly once he has spent his pleasure."

She blushed, something she did quite frequently when they discussed sexual matters and he kissed her to show his approval of her sweet innocence. He got sidetracked by her lips and it was several seconds before he again lifted his head.

"I want to watch you come apart, but if you continue to touch me, it will be me who loses control first."

"Why do you want to watch me?" she asked with genuine confusion and it was all he could do not to groan out loud.

"I cannot forget the way you shimmered like starlight in my arms yesterday. I want to see it again."

She still looked perplexed.

"It is a man thing," he said, in lieu of explaining why or how much sexual pleasure it gave him to watch her climax.

An impossible task.

"Okay." Her hand fell away from him and he bit back a groan of protest even while he shuddered with relief.

He kissed her and whispered against her lips, "Thank you."

She didn't say anything, her mouth opening on a silent scream as he kneaded her resilient flesh before pinching her swollen peak between his thumb and forefinger.

She arched off the blanket into his touch. "Damian, that feels *so good.*"

"Yes, it does." He caressed her again, his fingers deriving incredible pleasure from touching her gorgeous body. "You have the softest skin."

"Oh…"

Changing the pressure of his fingers, he watched carefully for signs of what she liked, but if her panting little moans were any indication, she liked it all. He moved his hand to the other breast and did the same thing and she started to rock against him, driving him crazy.

He wanted to touch her between her legs without the barrier of denim, but he knew he had to take things slow. He wanted her so mindless with pleasure when he caressed her down there that she accepted the touch without worrying he was going to try to penetrate her.

But he could touch the rest of her and he did, lightly tracing each of her ribs and running his fingertips along her collarbone and down between her breasts.

Her fingers were digging into his shoulders and she was kissing his neck, his chest, inhaling against the skin of his throat.

He drew circle after circle on each soft mound of her breasts, this time purposefully keeping his fingers away from her distended nipples. He wanted to see them. Nibbling on her earlobe, he started pulling her top off.

She grabbed the hem and held it down. "What are you doing?"

The nervous shake in her voice turned him on. It probably shouldn't, but it was like taking a virgin to bed for the first time and he liked it.

She hadn't been this nervous the day before, but that was probably because she'd had no time to think about what was happening between them. Passion had flared out of nowhere and he had been intent on burning past every barrier.

He traced her stiff fingers. "I want to see you."

"I'm too big."

"You are perfect."

When she didn't reply, he said, "You promised to trust me."

Her eyes widened and her lips parted, but then she nodded. Taking a deep breath that pressed her curves against his chest, she dropped her hands. She let him remove both her bra and top, leaving her upper torso completely bare to his hot gaze. Her nipples were deep red and turgid against the pale, creamy smoothness of her breasts.

"You are a work of art, Lia."

She choked on a sound and averted her face, while he devoured the sight of her large, but perfectly proportioned, tip-tilted breasts with his eyes. Then she did something unexpected. She looked at him, her face flushed with excitement, and leaned up on her elbows. Then she arched her back, displaying herself for his benefit.

"Lia..." He couldn't get enough air into his lungs to say more.

"I like you looking at me," she said shyly.

"I like to look…" He reached out with one hand and rolled his fingertip over and around the tip of each breast. "And I like to touch."

"So good…" Her head fell back in abandon and he lowered his so he could take one of the hard peaks in his mouth.

He sucked and she cried out, collapsing against the blanket again. He followed her, keeping his mouth on the succulent little berry.

He looked up, greedy for further evidence of her response and saw that she was biting the back of her hand. Muffled sounds came from her mouth that caused his erection to grow to painful magnitude in his jeans. He cupped her other breast and began to tug at its nipple as well.

Her head thrashed from side to side on the blanket, her hand now covering his own. "It's incredible. Damian… Just like yesterday…"

Unlike yesterday, today he would have her completely naked when he brought her to completion. He began stripping her out of her jeans. This time, she didn't make a peep of protest, not until he had to stop touching her to get rid of his own shirt. And then it was to complain about him moving away from her.

He left his jeans on, thinking she didn't need to see the extent of his arousal just yet.

He reached down and touched between her legs, this time without barriers. His finger slid easily between the slick folds of her feminine flesh, but he was careful not to stray past her clitoris.

Lia couldn't believe he was touching her so intimately and she was not freaking out. Maybe it was because she was too busy trying not to faint from pleasure. The way he was touching her, sent wave after wave of it through her body.

Without warning, he picked her up and rolled on his back at the same time. She ended up on top of him, her legs sprawled to the side. A large bulge pressed against the exposed flesh of her core and she couldn't help pushing herself more firmly against him.

He groaned.

She stilled. "Did I do something wrong?"

"No, *querida*. Only do it again."

She did.

"Sí. Perfecto."

They weren't exactly touching, not with his jeans between them, but the friction it created felt fantastic. It still wasn't enough, though, and she didn't know what to do to make it better.

"Damian, I…" Her voice faded into a high-pitched moan as he did something extraordinary to her nipple.

"What?" he asked against her ear, the warmth of his breath making her whole body quiver.

"I want more, but I don't know what to do."

"I do." Pressing against her derriere with one strong hand, he surged upward in a caress that sent shards of pleasure splintering through her.

But it was more intimate than she'd been with a man in over three years and she went tense, even though she didn't want to.

He rubbed her back in a soothing motion. "Don't get worried. I am still dressed. I will not hurt you. Trust me."

That word again. Trust. If she withheld it, she would only make it harder for both of them. Nodding in acknowledgement to his demand and her inner musings, she forced herself to relax.

"Sit up."

She didn't think she could, but he gently pushed her torso upward until she was straddling him like a horseback rider.

He spread his big hand against her spine. "Lean back."

She obeyed, shocked when the position made her rub against him in an incredibly exciting way. He rocked his hips and she gasped. Loud.

"Don't stop!" *It felt so good.*

"I could not. I have wanted you too long and now I will have you. I will not stop until we are both so exhausted from pleasure, sleeping will seem like it takes too much energy."

Warmth gushed between her legs at that diabolical promise.

He pulled her down a little so he could suckle her again, but this time they were connected intimately, if not joined and she convulsed without warning.

She screamed as her body bowed and her insides clenched in one almost vicious spasm after another. The explosion of pleasure going on inside her was so cataclysmic that their surroundings went fuzzy around the edges and then blackness claimed her.

When she came to, she was lying on the blanket with Damian leaning over her.

Her body was so languorous from pleasure, it was as if reality had completely receded and what she and Damian were doing was all that existed in the world.

"I want to see you," he said, his voice strained from un-spent passion. "All of you. And then I want to taste you."

"But—"

"Do you trust me, *mi esposa?*"

He kept calling her his wife and she was beginning to believe the title could be real. "Yes."

"Then, relax."

Lia lay quiescent as Damian moved into a kneeling position between her legs, pushing her thighs apart and her knees up. She had never been this open to a man, but Damian wanted to see her and after all the pleasure he had given her, she could not deny him.

Watching him look at her was unbearably arousing. His expression was so intent, so filled with desire.

But as his gaze grew hotter, she felt a familiar tight-ening inside her. Not this time. It wasn't fair. He'd given her so much pleasure, but her body would not cooper-ate. She knew that within seconds, even a cotton swab would not be able to penetrate her shrinking opening.

Tears burned her eyes.

He came down over her so his face was right above hers. "What is the matter, Lia?"

She averted her face. "It's happening."

"You mean the muscle contractions? Your body is closing?"

"*Yes.*" She tried to blink the tears away, but one slipped down her temple.

He brushed it away. "Does it hurt?"

"No." At least not physically. The sense she was not a complete woman devastated her emotions.

"Are you certain? You are not merely saying this to appease me?"

"Yes. It will only hurt if you try to go inside."

His smile was tinged with relief. "Then do not worry about it. We knew it was going to happen, *es verdad?*"

"Yes, but…"

He put his finger over her lips. "Shh…as long as you are not hurting, I do not want you even thinking about it, *comprendes?*"

He could not be for real. "But…"

"You promised me, Lia, your trust."

"I do trust you and I'll try not to think about it."

His eyes showered approval down on her, warming her insides as effectively as his touching did. Then he leaned down and kissed her until her body was involuntarily straining up toward his, seeking the contact of skin to skin.

She wrapped her arms around him, reveling in the feel of his hot strength beneath her fingers.

She moaned when he broke the kiss, but he moved down her body again, kissing and licking her *everywhere.* The things he did to her belly button made her cry out in both fear and pleasure. It was too much.

She tried to tell him, but he shook his head, his eyes filled with knowing. "I have barely begun."

Then he was kneeling between her legs. "I'm going to touch you, but that is all. I will not attempt penetration even with my fingertip, all right?"

She nodded, incapable of speech. It took more courage than he could ever know to let him touch her there, to believe he wouldn't hurt her, even accidentally. But she did believe him.

He traced her with his fingertip, but just as he promised, he made no attempt to press his finger into her tightly closed passage. "Were you aware that your outer tissue has more nerve endings and is therefore more sensitive than your inner tissue?"

"No." She could barely get the one word out past the tightness in her throat.

He continued touching her, building up a nameless need inside her until she was gyrating against his fingers.

She'd never known such wantonness, or such need. "Damian!"

He smiled, all sexy, primordial male. "What do you want? This?" And he brushed her sweet spot.

Just once, then again…and again.

The pleasure was more intense than anything she'd ever known. No one had touched her like he was touching her.

He knew exactly how much pressure to exert, how long to linger, what direction to move his fingers, what type of movement to use and when. It was mind-boggling, incredible, physically devastating.

He amazed her.

"Please…" He couldn't consummate, but he had to do something and she trusted him to do it.

He cupped her most secret place, like he was protecting her with his hand and what that did to her heart, she could not even bear to contemplate. Then he circled her clitoris with his thumb. Once. Twice. Three times and the tension coiling tight in her body threatened to spring.

"I must taste you."

That was all the warning she got before his head delved between her legs and his tongue took the place of his thumb.

She called his name, her voice thready with need and a fear she was desperately trying not to feel.

But his tongue did not trespass flesh too tight to accommodate it. He laved her most secret place tenderly and her legs closed of their own accord, trapping his head between them. He didn't seem to mind as he ministered to every millimeter of the soft, swollen flesh between her legs.

He even gently licked the seam of her stubbornly closed opening, but he didn't attempt to push his tongue inside. She shuddered with excitement. He'd been right. She was very sensitive there.

And he did exactly what he said he'd wanted to do. He tasted her.

She arched her pelvis upward, pressing herself to his mouth. "Damian, I can't stand it! *It's too much.* You've got to do something…"

He slid his hands between her legs, pushing her thighs apart just as if she wasn't trying to push them together as hard as she could. His strength would have astonished her if she wasn't already so dazzled by his prowess at loving. Exerting pressure until her muscles were stretched just this side of pain, he relentlessly opened her body completely to his questing mouth.

He kissed her swollen, slick flesh with his tongue until she was straining against the hold of his hands on her thighs and her fingers were buried in his hair, pulling and pushing from one second to another. Then he took her highly sensitized, swollen nub between his teeth and sucked.

She shattered into a million bitty pieces, her scream echoing around them. Bucking against the tongue that would not still, mini tremors shook her body, keeping every muscle in her body tense. She began to sob. The pleasure was just too much.

"Damian, please!"

He lifted his mouth and she collapsed back onto the blanket covered sand. Her body trembled from head to foot.

He kissed the inside of both of her thighs and then her now damp curls with his lips. "*Querida*, you are amazing."

She had to touch him and brushed his temple with her fingers. "You're the incredible one. That was… There are no words for what you just gave me."

He turned his head and kissed the center of her palm. "I am glad."

Her body all of a sudden bowed again, her muscles going into momentary rigor before she fell back again. "Damian, what's happening to me?"

"Do not worry. You flew very high and your body needs to come down." Then he pressed another kiss to her thighs.

Moving up her body, gentling the volcanic vibrations of her body with his mouth, he let her calm down until her breathing was almost back to normal. She tried to sit up, but he pressed her back down. It didn't take much. Her muscles were still rubbery from exertion.

But she needed to touch him. "I want…"

He kissed the words from her mouth.

After several long moments of pure pleasure with his mouth molding hers, he lifted his head. "I want to lie on top of you and make love to your body, but I need you to trust me not to attempt intercourse."

By giving her pleasure with no thought to his own,

not once, but twice, he'd more than proven that she could trust him with her femininity and her limitations. "I trust you, Damian."

His jaw locked and he kissed her, hard.

Then he stood up and stripped out of his jeans, revealing his straining desire to her hungry and curious gaze. He let her look for several seconds before coming down on top of her. He aligned their flesh as it had been before when she was straddling him, but this time the barrier of his jeans was not there. She forced herself to remain relaxed as he moved against her.

And soon, it became easier as he made no move to attempt penetration and the pleasure and tension grew inside her once again. She locked her hands behind his neck and twisted her legs around his, opening herself to him as completely as it was possible for *her* to do. She pushed her pelvis upward to increase the friction, moving with Damian in an age-old rhythm that they made uniquely theirs.

Damian felt himself losing control. Her trusting acquiescence sent him straight into oblivion and he pistoned against her, not even caring that he could not be inside her.

He felt his body going rigid, the pressure building, and then he was exploding with nuclear proportions. Incredibly she was crying out with him, straining her body toward his. They both collapsed at the same time.

"That was miraculous," she whispered against his neck and then kissed him.

He moved his mouth over hers, savoring the sweet, softness of her lips for as long as he dared, but when he felt the renewal of arousal, he stopped. "I had better move before I crush you."

"But this feels good."

It did. Too good, but she was not up to another round of lovemaking. He got up, pulling her with him and then carried her down to the surf where he insisted on washing her. Even after their intimate touching, it embarrassed her and she blushed.

"Your innocence fascinates me, but this blush…" He ran his finger from her cheek down her throat and over her flushed breasts. "It is *very* interesting."

"Stop that," she said breathlessly, but she was smiling and he grinned back.

He felt lighthearted, full of hope. It was not a feeling he trusted, but he would enjoy it while it lasted. "I've never seen a woman blush with her whole body before," he teased.

She grimaced and averted her face. "You've probably never gone to bed with a twenty-four-year-old woman who has less sexual experience than most seniors in high school, either."

Her vulnerability was every bit as charming as her innocence. "I like knowing that for all intents and purposes, you were practically a virgin."

Her mouth opened, but nothing came out and then she swung around and faced him, her expression filled with shocked disbelief. *"I wasn't a virgin."*

"You had never found the ultimate pleasure with a man before yesterday. That is a type of virginity. I am unashamedly glad to have had the privilege of initiating you."

"Initiating me? You're a real Neanderthal in some ways, you know that?"

They were standing waist deep in water and he liked

how he could see the shadow of her feminine secrets below the crystal clear water. "*Sí.*"

"You're not the least embarrassed to be so primitive?"

"Why should I be? Tobias Kennedy was probably more New Man than I will ever want to be, but he was not the one to teach you the secrets of your body."

He watched her temper flare with satisfaction. She was not nervous around him in her nakedness and he liked that.

"You are so arrogant." The words barely left her mouth before she splashed him right in the face.

The splashing fight that ensued left her panting and laughing and him feeling as if he'd touched something incredibly precious inside himself that he had forgotten was there.

CHAPTER SEVEN

LIA lounged on the blanket, dressed again, hair a wet tousle around her face. Damian had put his jeans back on, but left his bronze chest bare. They'd eaten the picnic he'd had in the backpack he brought down to the beach, but a companionable silence had fallen since they finished eating.

Which was a little surprising. Not only had he taken all her preconceived notions about her complete lack of sexuality and shredded them, but he threatened to do more. His demand she try to make love completely and give him the children her initial promise implied set her up for more heartbreak and failure down the road.

And yet right now, she was…happy. She had satisfied her husband and that felt very, very good, she realized.

"Grandfather said your family is from this area," she said, wanting to know more about him and wishing she didn't.

He was a dangerous threat to her emotional well-being.

His eyes turned cold and remote, shocking her with

the speed with which his mood could change. "They are."

"None of them were at the wedding."

"I told you, they do not acknowledge me."

Her grandfather had said the same thing, but she hadn't realized how total was her husband's status as persona non grata with his relatives. "None of them?"

"Not one. It is why I left Spain in the first place, but I did well going to New York to make my fortune."

"Was it hard leaving everything you knew behind?"

"No. After the courts denied my claim to my father's title, I wanted to get away from Spain and everything the country of my birth represented."

"How old were you when your father died?"

"Sixteen."

"I was fifteen when my daddy died. It was awful. I missed him so much."

"I cannot say the same. I'd never known Don Escoto, but I grew up knowing who he was, what I came from, what I should have been."

"Why did you sue for the title?"

"It was mine by right." It was hard to believe this remote stranger was the same man who had touched her so intimately earlier.

"But you are...."

"Illegitimate. *Sí.* I am this, however I was also the oldest child of my father."

"And titles are transferred by right of progenitor."

"Don Escoto's family denied his paternity to me. It was ridiculous. Everyone, including the judge who tried my case knew I was his son, but without proof, I had no case."

"Why didn't you have the DNA tests done, or something?"

"I was sixteen. I had no resources. Mama had no resources. The Escoto family had the money to drag the case out for years. I could not stand the thought of my mother losing everything to pursue what should have been mine without a fight. For years, I dreamed of accumulating enough wealth to challenge my younger sister for the title."

"Why didn't you?" He'd certainly gotten rich enough.

"My mother died and I realized that revenge would not give me what I wanted."

Such a stark statement, but so powerful.

"What *do* you want?"

"A sense of family."

"I can't give you a family, either."

"You already have. You and Kaylee belong to me now."

But she knew a stepdaughter and wife who was incapable of truly making love would not be enough for a man like Damian. She said nothing however, already regretting spoiling the rapport that had existed between them since their intimacy.

Instead she changed the subject. "Speaking of Kaylee... I didn't expect to spend the entire two weeks here and I'm not comfortable being apart from her right now."

Some of the tension drained out of him. "I anticipated this and had my car sent for her after our initial discussion this morning. She is no doubt already at the villa being acquainted with Juana and Carlos."

* * *

Which turned out to be exactly the case when Lia and Damian hiked back up to the house. They found Kaylee in the kitchen, helping Juana roll pastry for dinner.

She grinned up at her mother, her blue eyes dancing, her face flushed with enjoyment. "Mama, Señora Juana is letting me help her, see?" She pointed to her flour covered self and the misshapen pastry dough on the smooth wood tabletop in front of her.

Lia grinned, trying not to laugh. Kaylee was just so darn cute in Juana's apron, which had to be wrapped around twice to fit her. "I see. What are you two making?"

"*Empeñadas,* Mama. We get to put cherries in them."

Since her daughter's favorite food in the entire world was cherries in any shape or form, Juana couldn't have picked anything better to break the ice with the little girl.

"Sounds yummy."

"*Sí.*" Damian came up beside her and put his hand on her waist in a casual gesture of possessiveness.

Kaylee's smile stretched across her whole face. "You are my papa now, aren't you, Señor Damian?"

"*Sí.* You can call me Papa instead of Señor, do you not agree?"

"*Sí.*" Kaylee drew the word out in a long drawl and then hurled herself at Damian, who caught her in a bear hug, flour covered apron and all.

Lia wouldn't be the only one devastated when Damian decided to walk away. She wished she could change that, but she couldn't. She had bought Kaylee's life with a set of circumstances guaranteed to bring them both emotional pain, but Kaylee would survive that. She would not survive the hole in her heart. Their course had been set and it had to be run, no matter what the outcome.

Damian insisted on bringing in a leading heart surgeon to consult on Kaylee's case. The doctor was affiliated with a well-known institute in Seattle where researchers were on the forefront of treatment for heart disease.

Damian arranged for Kaylee and Lia to accompany him on his private jet to Seattle six days after the wedding.

Kaylee, who loved air travel anyway, adored the opportunity to go on a private plane and was ecstatic when the pilot allowed her up front to watch him fly the plane.

Damian sat down beside Lia, heaving a sigh. "Where does one tiny body come up with so much energy?"

"I don't know. I think it shows God's sense of humor. He matches exhausted parents with inexhaustible children."

Damian turned toward her, all sensual predatory male. "You did not feel exhaustible to me last night."

Remembering all they had done in the dark warmth of the night, she blushed. "You're the one who doesn't seem to have an off button."

He laughed, a low, tigerish chuckle and bent close to her, breathing in her scent, surrounding her with his. "And would you be happy if I did, *mi esposa?*"

"No, Damian. You are an amazing man, in and out of the bedroom." The words slipped out unbidden, but she would not take them back if she could.

He had shown himself to be two men. One a ruthless negotiator who demanded she keep her side of an unholy bargain. The other a charming companion who had stolen her daughter's heart and was making a major dent in her own. Perhaps Damian was as her grandfather had said, only ruthless when he needed to be.

She was doing what he wanted and he rewarded her and Kaylee with consideration and kindness. She liked it.

"*Sí*…the spa bath was fun, was it not?"

She choked on a laugh. "I didn't mean tha—"

He cut her off with his lips and then she lost all will to attempt to communicate on any level but this one.

Damian checked his new family into a corporate apartment style hotel with two bedrooms and an office. Lia would appreciate the privacy and homelike atmosphere, but it also had the benefit of daily maid service should he choose to pay for it. He, of course, paid.

He wanted everything as easy for Lia as possible and told her so when she questioned the maid service scheduled for the next morning after they had settled Kaylee in to sleep. His new daughter had wanted him to read her bedtime story and he had put off an international business call to do it. He'd made the call and now wanted to see his wife.

He went in search of her and found her in the kitchen. She was wearing a caramel colored satin robe that reached her toes. The soft lighting from the stove's overhead light cast the valleys and curves of her luscious body in shadow.

Desire, hot and urgent, swept through him with tidal wave force. That body belonged to him just as the woman belonged to him. Did she realize it yet? Did she understand that whatever the deal had been, now she was his?

She looked up from a pot she was stirring on the stove, her amber eyes warm with welcome. "I made some hot cocoa, do you want some?"

"Hot cocoa?"

She grinned and nodded. "You know that stuff you make with cocoa powder, cream, sugar and some other stuff that if I told you, I'd be in danger of losing my reputation as the Queen of Cocoa Making."

"Heaven forbid such a thing would happen."

She was so different from the other women he had had in his life. She did not act like a woman raised with privilege, the granddaughter of a wealthy *conde*.

"Kaylee would be devastated. I've promised to pass the recipe down to her on her sixteenth birthday."

He moved so he could look over her shoulder and take a whiff of the aroma coming from the pot. The decadent richness of the chocolate competed with the soft, feminine scent he knew to be hers and hers alone.

He nuzzled her neck. "It smells good."

"It, or me?" she asked with a catch in her voice that never failed to turn him on.

"Both, *querida,* both." He kissed her neck and she shivered. "I smell sensual, sweet woman, chocolate and cinnamon."

She tilted her head back, put her finger to her lips and widened her eyes in exaggerated concern. "Shhh… That's one of the secret ingredients."

"Is it?"

"Well, lots of people use cinnamon, but they use the

powder, not dried chips." She went back to stirring, letting her head rest back against his chest.

No longer did she respond to his nearness like a wary doe to the hunter and it pleased him.

She turned off the burner with a flick of her wrist. "Now you know one of my secrets."

"One day, I will know all your secrets, *querida,* then watch out."

"You already know the ones I've hidden from everyone else in the world." She sounded resigned to that reality rather than pleased by it.

She was still bothered by her sexual limitations and he did not know how to help her accept them. It had to be obvious he enjoyed their sensual intimacy as much, or more, than she did, but still she saw herself as defective.

She was not defective, but he was not convinced her condition was untreatable. Both she and her first husband had been naïve and embarrassed by the challenges her body presented; they would not have felt comfortable pursuing a medical remedy.

He hoped that reticence on her part was diminished because his initial research indicated he was right to believe there were treatments available. He had plans to consult with a specialist in sexual dysfunction while they were in Seattle as well as the cardiologist for Kaylee.

"Do you mind me knowing you so intimately?" he asked.

She didn't answer for a long time and when she did, her voice was thoughtful. "No. You took my secret and changed it. I thought I could not share any sort of sexual pleasure with you and you've taught me differently." She paused as if preparing herself to say something difficult. "I know I haven't said it, but thank you."

Her gratitude made him uncomfortable and he moved away. "You have no need to thank me. The passion is shared between us and giving you pleasure is my privilege."

She busied herself pouring the hot cocoa, but the slight downturn of her mouth indicated his withdrawal had bothered her.

He found himself wanting to explain, when explanations of any kind were usually an anathema to him. "I was almost married twice for the things I could give."

Her head lifted and serious amber eyes probed straight into his soul. "What happened?"

"I was twenty-two when I made my first million. I underwrote a start-up venture with capital I had amassed from other sources, convincing men like your grandfather to invest in the business. It took off and I'm still getting residual income on the investment, but success carried a price. Most of the people around me wanted something. I made the mistake of believing Crystal was different. Your grandfather revealed her duplicity to me, much to the devastation of my pride."

"Did you love her?"

"I thought so at the time, but I realized later I loved the woman she had pretended to be…the one I wanted her to be, not the woman she was. It was a sobering experience, but still I did not learn my lesson."

"You got suckered a second time?" Lia asked, sounding shocked.

And well she might be. He wasn't proud of the fact

he had been so stupid, not once, but twice in his life. "*Sí*. This time by a woman in the Spanish nobility."

"You were susceptible because you were still looking for acceptance."

"You are perceptive."

"I suppose Grandfather revealed this woman's duplicity to you as well."

"No, but he told me he suspected she wanted my money and not me. I had her background investigated and discovered her father faced bankruptcy. Had she been honest about her circumstances, I would not have cared. But that's not why I left her. She had something I wanted and I would have married her to get it."

"An entrée into the society your father's ignoring you denied you."

"As I said, you are perceptive, but she was also the oldest child and would inherit the title, a title that would pass on to my children."

"You know, you've spent years living in the States, I'm surprised you're still so impacted by what is essentially an empty name you get to sign on legal documents."

He shrugged and leaned against the counter beside where she stood. "I am still very much a Spaniard at heart."

In other words, it was a matter of his pride. "I guess you've got pretty much the same deal with me."

"*Sí,* but this time Benedicto sought approval of a special dispensation to assign one of his lesser titles to me during my lifetime. The king granted the dispensation the day before our wedding."

"So, what…you are now *Don* Marquez?"

"*Sí.*"

"And that makes you happy?"

He shrugged. Happy? "I am satisfied with it."

She nodded. "I see."

"The title of Papa given me by Kaylee gives me far more satisfaction," he said, admitting a surprising truth.

She scooped a fluffy white dollop of whipped cream onto each of the mugs of cocoa and then grated some chocolate on top. "You were born to be a father, Damian."

The flat tone of her voice bothered him. "Are you again worried about not being able to give me more children?"

"You can't pretend it doesn't matter." She handed him one of the warm mugs. "It's part of the package you thought you were getting. You want your child to have the title and place in Spanish society you were denied."

He couldn't deny her words, but if the worst happened and she could not conceive his child, he would not abandon her because of it. The knowledge did not surprise him. He was, after all a fair man. She was doing her best to keep her side of their bargain and he would keep his.

"So what happened with your second big romance?" she asked in an obvious bid to change the subject.

"Juliana was in love with another man, one she eloped with after I caught them together kissing in the kitchen."

"In the kitchen?"

"He was her father's chef."

"His chef? You've got to be kidding."

"No."

"I bet he didn't make hot cocoa as good as this stuff."

She touched his cup with hers in a universal toasting gesture, her amber gaze filled with an invitation to share the joke.

He tipped the cup to his lips, letting the smooth, rich chocolate slide across his tongue. "You are right. It is delicious."

She wiped her brow with the back of her hand, her expression teasing. "Whew. I was worried I might not impress you with my cocoa making skills."

No woman had ever teased him so much before.

"Do not worry, such skills are only one of the many things about you that impresses me."

She smiled and took a sip, leaving a swath of white cream on her upper lip when she put the cup down.

"You have a cream mustache."

"Do I?" she asked with batting eyelashes, all provocative innocence. "Maybe you'd like to clean me up?"

Although she responded beautifully in their bed, she rarely took the initiative. It did strange things to his heart to realize his feelings were important enough to her to step outside her comfort zone to make him feel better.

He leaned down until his mouth was only a breath from her own. "I believe I would like that very much."

She was everything he had thought she would be and more, but was that because she was coming to care for him? Her generous affection in and out of the bedroom could be the result of so many things…her gratitude over what he was doing for Kaylee, her guilt at tricking him into marriage under false pretenses or a simple physical reaction to the passionate pleasure he gave her.

His thoughts splintered as her tongue came out to mesh with his, licking the sweet cream from her sweeter lips.

Kaylee's appointment with the heart surgeon went extremely well. His kindness and warmth made the little girl comfortable and Lia was grateful. She didn't want her daughter terrified by what she was facing. Lia was scared enough for both of them and doing her best to hide it. It helped her so much that Damian had made time to attend the doctor's appointment with them.

The surgeon confirmed what the doctor in New Mexico had said regarding Kaylee's condition, but the procedure he suggested was not anywhere near as invasive or risky as open heart surgery.

When Lia asked why, the doctor explained that not all hospitals paid for the privilege of using surgical techniques other doctors had patented. This doctor had been performing a new procedure for the last two years with a great deal of success. It took about an hour and had one-sixth the recovery time of open heart surgery. It was only available for certain types of heart disease, but the hole in Kaylee's heart was one of them.

The surgeon had a nurse come in and take Kaylee for a dish of ice cream in the hospital cafeteria.

"We can schedule the procedure as early as next week," he said after the two had left.

"And she will only have to remain in the hospital for a couple of days?"

"Her activity will be limited for a certain time, but she will be quite safe going home."

"Can we fly her back to New York?" Damian asked.

"That should not pose a problem, but I would let her convalesce in Seattle for three or four days before taking any plane trips."

"No problem."

Lia smiled. That was Damian's approach to everything. No problem. He made things happen. She had gotten a lot more out of their marriage deal than money, she'd gotten a man she could rely on. The fact she wanted to worried her a little, but she was so tired of being independent.

He scheduled the surgery and hospital stay while she and Kaylee explored the cardiac center.

"Mama, am I gonna have surgery?"

"Yes, baby, but then you'll be all better."

"And you won't cry anymore when you think I'm sleeping?"

Lia dropped to her knees and took her daughter into her arms, trying hard to stop herself from hugging the breath right out of her, but not sure she succeeded when Kaylee squeaked. "I won't cry anymore. I'm sorry you heard me before, butterfly."

"It's okay, Mama. I love you."

"I love you, too."

They were back at their temporary apartment and Kaylee was watching a cartoon when Damian broached the subject of contacting Lia's grandfather.

"Call him if you like, but I have nothing to say to him." She hadn't forgiven or forgotten that he'd used her daughter's illness to manipulate her into marriage with Damian. She'd needed her grandfather and instead of being there for her, he used the situation to his own advantage. Maybe he hadn't had the money to help, but using that lack to push her in a direction he wanted her to go was unconscionable.

He had said it that day in his study. He hadn't *wanted* to look for alternatives. He had wanted her to marry Damian.

"Benedicto only wants what is best for you."

"Blackmailing me with my daughter's health is not best for me."

"But the results are not so bad, surely?"

She shook her head, knowing she didn't know how to explain to Damian that in this case, the ends, no matter how wonderful, did not justify the means. And she wasn't sure they would all be fantastic, was she? She had been happier in the last few days than she'd been in her whole life, but she was just waiting for the roof to cave in on that happiness.

When it did, Kaylee was going to be hurt, too, and she might have to accept that, but she didn't have to like it.

Every night Damian took her on a sensual journey that left her exhausted and sated with pleasure. However, she could never forget the fact that her condition made it impossible for her to give him the children he craved. It weighed on her mind, tingeing even the most incredible lovemaking with a sense of impermanency.

"Our marriage has been surprisingly good so far," she said, unable to lie or tell the complete truth—that she was just waiting for him to walk. It would offend him, especially if he had convinced himself he was in it for the long haul.

"So you still see yourself as a victim of your grandfather's scheming and my insistence you keep your word?" he asked, his expression unreadable.

His cell phone rang before she could answer, not that she was sure she knew what she would have said.

She was still angry with Grandfather, but that anger did not extend to her husband. Probably because she knew he thought he would stay married to her. He didn't know that years of incomplete sex would eventually take their toll. They had to.

She watched him walk away with a strange feeling in her heart. If she didn't know better, she might think she was falling in love with the impossible man.

He found her later in the living room watching a re-run of *I Love Lucy*. "Are you ready for bed, *mi mujer?*"

She looked up. "I really like being your woman." That at least was one truth she could openly admit.

He lifted her high in his arms and carried her to the bathroom where she found herself taking a very erotic shower. Then he swept her off to bed to make love to her all over again. She was in the throes of frenzied passion when she felt his finger gently press inside her. He slid it in to the first knuckle and exultation like nothing she'd ever known coursed through her.

However, even as the joy flashed into her wounded heart, her flesh betrayed her again, closing around his finger with vise-like intensity.

Tears filled her eyes and her entire body shook with a violent sob. "I can't do it!"

He gently withdrew, oh so careful not to hurt her and

she tried to turn on her side to curl into a fetal ball. She just wanted to give in and stop trying to be strong.

He wouldn't let her. One hand caught her shoulder and the other her hip, holding her in place. "I am not done with you."

"I'm defective, Damian! We both know it. What's the use?"

"I want you, Lia."

"How can you?"

He didn't bother to speak, didn't feed her the platitudes Toby had done right up until he asked for the divorce. Damian was too honest for that, but he was also determined. He started to kiss her again, stoking the fires of her passion with his hands until she forgot her defeat and could only think of the way he made her feel.

Which was incredible.

CHAPTER EIGHT

THE next few days flew by with Damian, Lia and Kaylee seeing the sights of Seattle while they waited for the day for her procedure to arrive. The day before it was scheduled, Damian had business that required him leaving Lia and Kaylee.

"I thought this was our honeymoon," Lia complained, pouting for maybe the first time in her life.

He smiled and kissed her mouth with its protruding lip until she melted against him in a boneless mass of feminine submission. "It is a small thing and I will not be gone very long, *querida.*"

She sighed, soaking in the certainty that burned down at her from his dark eyes. He was a multimillionaire business tycoon, and sometimes that business was going to take precedence. "I guess I should be grateful you're here with me at all. I'm sure there's a lot of stuff in New York that could do with your personal attention."

Her grandfather would never have spent so many weeks away from the base of his business operations.

"I would never be so remiss as to leave you to face this ordeal with Kaylee alone, you must know this."

Remiss. A word connected to duty and responsibility. A cold chill swept down her spine and she stepped away. "Yes, of course."

She could not start believing he did any of this out of a newfound affection or caring. He was simply once again keeping up his end of the bargain. He did it so darn well, she almost fooled herself into believing he cared sometimes. Why she wanted to do such a foolish thing, she refused to even contemplate.

"Maybe I'll take Kaylee shopping."

His eyes searched hers. "That sounds like a good idea, and do not hesitate to buy something if you like it."

She'd spent so long on an economy budget that she had a hard time remembering she could now afford to splurge a little. Damian had noticed her tendency not to buy things for herself when they visited The Museum of Natural Science and she had found a hand soldered glass kaleidoscope she liked. She'd put it down after exclaiming over it and he had presented it to her as a gift when they reached the car.

She smiled wryly. "Don't worry. I think I can get the hang of spending money indiscriminately."

He laughed and shook his head. "I doubt it, but I would not mind."

And she knew he told the truth. Damian took his role as her husband very seriously. It was all part of fulfilling his side of the bargain completely.

They hit one of Seattle's bigger malls and did the toy stores first, delighting Kaylee when she found the doll to go with her favorite movie.

They were walking by Victoria's Secret when Lia stopped to stare at a very daring, very sexy basque in the window.

"Mama, that lady's underwear is really pretty," Kaylee said pointing at the mannequin.

Lia agreed. She'd never worn sexy underthings because Toby would have considered them a painful form of teasing. After her marriage ended, she hadn't felt like highlighting her sexuality in any way. Things were different with Damian, even if it was temporary and she was positive he would appreciate the effort. She took Kaylee's hand and led her into the lingerie store.

Damian waited impatiently for Lia and Kaylee to return from their shopping expedition. He'd called her cell phone a half an hour ago and been told they were on their way home. Lia had also said she'd bought a surprise for him. It was ridiculous, but he couldn't wait to see what it was. He could not remember the last time a woman had bought him anything, or anyone else for that matter. Not since his mother's death anyway.

He heard the snick of a lock and the click of a door latch a second before a small blond dynamo came rushing into the room.

Kaylee threw herself against Damian, hugging him and planting a baby-girl kiss right on his cheek. "We had the bestest time shopping. Mama got me a doll and she bought you something too, Papa."

He loved the sound of that name on the small child's lips. "She told me, *niña*. I look forward to seeing it."

"Do you want to see my new doll, too?"

"Of course."

Kaylee dropped to the floor and opened the bag she'd been carrying. She pulled out a doll dressed like a medieval princess with very long blond hair. "Isn't she pretty?"

"*Sí*, but not as lovely as my new daughter or her mama."

Kaylee giggled, her blue eyes twinkling with happiness Damian hoped would never be diminished.

"Flattery will get you your present before dinner instead of after." Lia came into the room and straight to him just as Kaylee had done.

However, instead of a peck on the cheek, she pressed her lips to his in a lingering salute that made him wish their daughter was not so full of energy and they did not have company meeting them for dinner.

When she pulled back, her amber eyes glowed with an unfamiliar mischievous sparkle. "Let me put the bags in the bedroom and I'll dig out your present."

He had a better idea and he tugged her into his lap. "You can 'dig it out' here, I think."

She smiled, her expression filled with a delight he could become addicted to. "All right."

She dropped all the bags but one onto the floor beside him. When he saw a familiar pink and white bag, his body reacted instantly as images of her wearing something from that store flitted through his mind.

"Is my present in there?" he asked, pointing to the bag.

"No, silly, that's stuff for Mommy. You can't wear it," Kaylee said before her mother could get a single word out.

"I wonder." He touched his wife's petal soft, pinkened cheek. "If it is not for me, then why are you blush-ing?"

"Don't tease, or I won't give you your other present."

"Ah, so that one is for me."

"You know it is…in a way anyway."

He could no more resist kissing her than he could have prevented himself taking his next breath. She was fast becoming every bit as necessary to his well-being as well.

When he lifted his head, Lia was breathing in an ir-regular pattern and Kaylee was talking to her doll. "I guess they're gonna do that a lot, but they sure stay at it longer than you did in the movie."

Lia's laugh preceded his by only a nanosecond. Then she handed a small bag to him.

"My present?"

"Yes."

He opened the bag and pulled out a compact disc of one of his favorite artists. "It is the new album." He had not realized it had hit the stores yet.

"I saw his other ones in the stereo cabinet at the villa. It just came out in stores yesterday. I took a chance on you not having it preordered."

"I did not."

She sighed happily and relaxed against him as if it were the most natural thing in the world for her to do. "I'm glad." She rubbed her cheek against his chest. "I'm so tired, I could sleep for a week. Do you mind if we order dinner in tonight?"

"I am sorry, *querida,* but we have plans."

Her head came up. "Plans? You didn't say anything this morning."

For the simple reason that Benedicto had not seen fit to apprise Damian of his and Maria-Amelia's trip to Seattle until they were already checked into a downtown hotel. They wanted to be with Lia during Kaylee's procedure.

"I didn't know about them this morning."

"Oh. Is it business? There won't be any problem with Kaylee coming will there? I really hate the idea of putting on a dress and makeup. You're going to owe me big time."

"There is no problem with Kaylee coming because it is not business. You can stay in your current outfit and I will change our reservations to a more casual restaurant." He liked her in her jeans and lace patterned T-shirt that showed just the tiniest bit of her tummy above her waistband when she moved.

"If it's not business, what is it? If you're thinking to take us out to relax before tomorrow, I'd rather just stay here and I'm sure Kaylee would, too."

He had suspected that was the case, but he also believed she would be more comfortable entertaining her family at a restaurant than in the apartment.

A peremptory knock sounded on the door as he said, "Your mother and grandfather have flown over."

Lia jumped off his lap. "Grandfather is here?"

"*Sí.* If I am not mistaken, at our door as we speak."

She looked at the door like an evil genie resided on the other side. "You invited my grandfather here?" she asked, her voice laced with accusation.

"It was not exactly—"

Another series of knocks cut him off.

Damian answered the door when he realized Lia had no intention of letting her grandfather and mother in.

When he led them back to the living room, Kaylee was its only occupant. Lia and all the shopping bags were gone.

Kaylee got up from the carpet to hug her grandmother and great-grandfather and show them her new doll. She kept a steady flow of childish chatter up for several minutes, until Benedicto asked, "Where is Rosalia?"

"She and Kaylee just arrived from their shopping trip. She is putting things away in our bedroom."

"Surely it can wait."

Privately, Damian thought so, too, but Lia's unpleasant surprise at her grandfather's arrival probably had more to do with her longer than expected absence than anything else. He was just about to go and see if she ever planned to join them when she walked into the room.

She was wearing a black dress and the despised makeup. Her hair had been brushed to a glossy flip around her neatly composed face.

She walked directly up to her mother and hugged her. "Hello, Mama. This is a surprise. I did not realize you planned to come to Seattle."

Maria-Amelia hugged her daughter back warmly. "I wanted to be here tomorrow." She looked at Kaylee, her gaze which Damian had often thought vague, focused with intense emotion on her granddaughter.

"Of course, we are here. You should not have expected anything different." At the sound of Benedicto's voice, Lia tensed, but she pasted a social smile on her face and turned to face him.

"Grandfather, thank you for bringing Mama over." Her lack of overt welcome toward the older man was obvious to everyone in the room but Kaylee.

The little girl's smile went undimmed as she held her grandmother's hand.

"I wished to be here as well, Rosalia."

She shrugged and looked down at her daughter. "Are you ready for dinner? Maybe we should fuss you up a little."

"Okay, Mommy, but do I have to wear tights?" she asked in such a plaintive tone that it was all Damian could do not to laugh.

Like mother, like daughter.

"You may wear pants. How about your new purple outfit with the kitties on it?"

Benedicto's harrumph of disapproval was drowned out by Maria-Amelia's suggestion she help her granddaughter dress.

Lia accepted the help, but went with them, making it very clear she had no desire to remain in the company of her grandfather...or her husband.

"You said the two of you were getting along."

"We are."

"Then why is she still so angry with me?"

Damian didn't have an answer for the other man. If Lia was happy married to him, why hold a grudge against her grandfather?

On the other hand, "You hurt her when you used Kaylee's illness as a weapon to get what you wanted."

"Does she think I could have manufactured the money out of thin air?" he asked in an aggrieved tone.

But Damian just looked at the other man and Benedicto had the grace to look uncomfortable. "All right, I could have made it happen without our bargain, but I wanted you two married damn it. And by all accounts it's working, so why hold a grudge? You didn't."

"You withheld information from me, you did not successfully manipulate me into doing something I did not want. Lia's pride is probably still smarting. She is your granddaughter after all."

"*Harrumph.*"

Damian had no desire to dwell on a reaction that indicated his wife was not nearly as content with her circumstances as he had believed before their surprise visitors arrived. He asked Benedicto about something related to business and refused to allow the conversation to return to Lia again.

Lia kicked off her shoes and unzipped her dress while she headed for the shower. Kaylee had fallen asleep on the way home from the restaurant and Damian had offered to put her to bed. Lia had gratefully accepted, so exhausted by an evening putting on a front of peaceful happiness when her feelings were anything but, undressing herself was almost beyond her.

Despite her fatigue, her mind was still whirling a mile a minute. Hopefully, a long, soothing shower during which she did little more than stand under the hot streams of water would relax her enough to sleep.

The sheath slid from her shoulders and she let it fall to the floor, uncaring that the laundry hamper was only two feet away. The panty hose took more effort and she snagged them in her clumsy efforts to peel them off. She threw them away with relish, using the last spark of energy in her body and then sagged down onto the vanity chair.

Did she even have enough energy to stand under the shower?

Her feet hurt from squeezing them into pumps while they were still swollen from her and Kaylee's shopping marathon. Her face hurt from forcing smiles she did not feel and her heart hurt because Damian obviously believed that she should have had no problem with her grandfather and mother's arrival.

She *didn't* have a problem with Mama wanting to be there when Kaylee had her procedure, but she found her grandfather's evinced concern hypocritical in the extreme.

"She didn't even wake up when I put her pajamas on her."

Lia looked up at the sound of Damian's voice. She still had her panties on, but that was all. For the first time in days, she felt uncomfortable in her seminudity around him and she grabbed a towel to wrap around her torso.

The movement was not lost on him and his dark brown eyes narrowed. "You are angry with me."

"How do you expect me to feel? You invited my grandfather here against my wishes."

"I did not invite him, he came on his own inclinations. However, I do not recall you stating a desire to the contrary."

She wasn't buying it. No way was he putting this back on her. "You had to know I wouldn't want him here, especially right now."

"It is right now that *he* needs to be here. He cannot wait a half a world away while his great-granddaughter's life hangs in the balance."

"And his feelings matter more to you than mine." If Damian loved her, *her* feelings would be paramount for him.

Like that was some surprise. Of course he didn't love her. They hadn't married for love and even if her feelings were growing, there was no reason to believe his ever would.

"I understand his feelings. I do not understand yours."

She couldn't believe he was that dense. Was it all men, or just tycoons that thought any road to Damascus would do, even one they had to bulldoze a village to build? "What's there not to understand? My grandfather threatened me with my daughter's life and that isn't something I can dismiss."

Damian frowned, his dark eyes both concerned and impatient. "Do not be melodramatic. He did not threaten Kaylee's life."

"What do you call refusing to pay for necessary surgery?"

"He never refused."

"He simply required I earn the money," she said with a bitter cynicism that shocked her.

It shocked him, too, if the expression on his too handsome face was any indication. "Do you consider our life together a series of payments on a debt you owe me?"

"I…"

"Do you respond to my passion with your own out of a sense of duty?"

"No." Duty could not ring that kind of response from her once deadened sensuality.

Damian nodded. "Do not talk of earning money in our marriage again."

"Fine, but that won't change what my grandfather did."

"Benedicto hurt you and this was wrong, but would you make him pay by refusing him the right to stand by you in your time of need?"

"He's not standing by me. This is about him needing to be here, you said so yourself."

"And you will dismiss this need because of what he did?"

"I am not dismissing his needs. I'm just not happy about having to deal with them on top of everything else."

He opened his mouth to speak, but she put up her hand to silence him. "Please don't say *anything else*. I'm tired. Really tired. I don't want to discuss my grandfather or anything else. Not Kaylee, not how you think I should feel differently…nothing. Even if you can't understand me, can you understand *that*?" She sounded every bit as weary and disillusioned as she felt.

"*Sí.*" All impatience drained from his expression, leaving only concern, but she didn't trust it.

She now knew that when it came to his concern for her and his concern for her grandfather, she came in a poor second. But then the two men had a long-term relationship built on mutual respect and business interests. What did she have with Damian? Passion and a sex life he would eventually grow weary of.

"I need a shower and then I'm going to bed."

He looked like he wanted to say more, but after a

long silence, he merely turned and left. She pushed the bathroom door shut after him, closing herself into a lonely isolation, something she'd known a lot of since her father died when she was fifteen. When she stepped into the steaming enclosure, she refused to dwell on the fact that her face was wet before the water even touched it.

They had to be at the hospital at 7:00 a.m. the next morning for anesthesia. Kaylee was brave, but Damian could tell she was nervous. Just as he could see the nervousness in her mother. However, unlike Kaylee, who had clung to both his and Lia's hand in the car ride over, Lia was intent on avoiding him.

She'd allowed Kaylee to sit between them in the car. He would have thought that normal under the circumstances, but she had been careful to avoid his physical proximity since arriving at the hospital as well.

Things only got worse after Kaylee was anesthetized and they went to the waiting room. Benedicto and Maria-Amelia were already there, seated in two chairs near the door. Lia drew into herself until Damian felt like she was not even in the waiting room with them.

"How long is the procedure supposed to take?" Benedicto asked.

Lia ignored the question, staring blankly ahead and leaving it for Damian to answer. "It could be done in as quickly as an hour."

"This is no fast-food restaurant. These doctors do not need to hurry. They should take their time. That is my great-granddaughter they are operating on."

"It is not technically an operation, Papa." Maria-Amelia darted a worried glance at her daughter after correcting her father. She'd obviously noticed Lia's withdrawal, too.

"Whatever it is, are you sure these are the best doctors for the job?" he demanded of Damian.

"*Sí.*"

"Humph!" Benedicto stood up and paced the room. "Operation or procedure, it is still damn nerve-racking having to wait for the results."

Lia stood up, and looking at no one, left the room.

She could be going to the bathroom, but somehow, Damian doubted it. He followed her, leaving a grumbling Benedicto and clearly stressed Maria-Amelia in the waiting room.

Lia was turning a corner when he came into the hall and in an outside courtyard when he caught up with her. "Why did you leave?"

"I want to be alone." She didn't look at him and that bothered him.

So did her desire for solitude. "You shouldn't be by yourself right now."

"It beats sitting around listening to my hypocrite of a grandfather espouse concern for my daughter's welfare and question decisions he wanted no part of."

"I did not ask his opinion."

"I did…or at least, I asked for his help and he gave me an ultimatum instead. He turned my daughter's welfare into a business proposition. He owed you and he willingly sacrificed me to assuage his pride."

Finally Damian was beginning to understand. Once, Benedicto had told him that Lia did not know the old man very well, but what he had neglected to mention was that what she did know…she did not trust.

"He did not encourage our marriage to benefit himself."

"Do you deny you have helped him out financially?"

"No."

"He offered me and all I represented to you as payment, isn't that right?"

"Lia, he wanted what was best for you, too. You must see that."

"I only see that he's been sponging off you for years, he saw a way to salvage his pride and he took it."

"It was not like that." He shook his head in frustration, wishing he could see her face, but not wanting to push her too far in her fragile emotional state. "He loves you, but you do not trust him at all."

Her body tensed as if under an intolerable burden. "How can I? He took me away from everything I knew after Daddy died."

"Surely that was your mother's decision."

"One she reached after a lecture on duty and her moral obligation to raise me among my family in Spain. But it wasn't enough to get us living under his roof, he had to control everything. He wouldn't even let me go home for a visit."

"That was shortsighted of him."

"Very." She spun to face him. "Do you really think I would have eloped with a boy I hadn't even seen in three years if I hadn't been desperate?"

"You had not seen Tobias Kennedy in three years?"

"No. The kiss we shared to seal our wedding vows was only the second one we'd ever had."

"I assumed you married in a passionate desire to be with the one your grandfather and mother denied you."

"They didn't even know about Toby. We kept in touch via e-mail and a handful of phone calls. I thought I loved him when I was fifteen. I was furious about having to move to Spain. I'd already lost the most important man in my life; I needed my best friend."

So many things became clear. "And yet the love of a friend is not necessarily the love needed to make a marriage work."

"According to you and my grandfather, love isn't a necessary ingredient at all."

He *had* believed that, but he was no longer so sure. He would like very much to believe she loved him.

"Hadn't you better get back to my grandfather? I'm sure he would appreciate your company." Her voice lacked any animation, but the accusation was there all the same and one thing became clear that he had not considered before.

She believed his relationship with Benedicto was more important to him than she was.

Damian cupped her shoulders, trying to impart some of his strength to the woman who had become intrinsically linked to his happiness. "The day after Kaylee joined us at the villa, I called Benedicto. I told him that what he had done was wrong and that I was furious with him for manipulating you with your daughter's health."

She shrugged, her shoulders moving jerkily under his hands. "So? It wasn't like you were willing to let me renege on my side of the deal."

"And would you be pleased now if I had done so?"

"That's not the point."

"In regard to me demanding you keep your word, that is exactly the point."

"Well, you and my grandfather have certainly made up now, so I'm not sure what point you were trying to make with that, either."

"He now understands that if he ever attempts to manipulate you or Kaylee in any way again, I will sever our relationship and dissolve the partnership. No matter how it happened, I am now married to the woman I want for my wife and I will protect you and our daughter always."

She seemed to stop breathing for a second.

"Lia?"

"Did you mean it?" she asked with a crack in her voice, her head bowed.

"*Sí*. Your grandfather knows me well. I do not bluff."

"And you really want me to be your wife?"

He carefully tilted her chin up and felt like he'd been kicked in the gut when he saw the tears on her face and wrenching uncertainty in her beautiful amber eyes. "*Sí*."

"You can't." She shook her head, her eyes closing in distress.

Now was not the time for the conversation, but he could cement her trust in him...show her that she came before her grandfather in his priorities. He pulled Lia close, kissing her temple and then her lips in a tender salute that held no hint of sexual need or desire.

She sighed and melted against him, wrapping her arms around his waist. "I'm so scared, Damian."

"Kaylee will be well. You will see."

She nodded against his chest, but she did not let go

and that is how the surgeon found them forty-five minutes later.

"Your daughter is in recovery, Mrs. Marquez."

Lia pulled away from Damian, but he kept one arm over her shoulders. "The procedure…"

"Was a complete success. In a very short while, your daughter will be recovered and as healthy as any other child her age."

Lia sagged against Damian. "I'm so glad." Her voice was a bare whisper. "How can I ever thank you?"

"Kaylee's health is all the thanks I need, Mrs. Marquez. She's a wonderful little girl."

"Yes, she is."

CHAPTER NINE

LIA walked into Kaylee's hospital room with her hand in Damian's.

He hadn't allowed her out of touching distance since coming out to her in the courtyard.

She sucked in a breath and blinked back tears. "Her body looks so small in that bed."

Kaylee's eyes slid open and a wan smile curled her tiny bow lips. "Hi, Mama. Hi, Papa."

They walked over to her and took turns hugging her carefully and kissing her baby soft cheeks.

"I'm sleepy," she said as they both straightened to stand beside her bed.

"It is the anesthesia, *niña*."

"It will wear off soon and then you'll feel better," Lia promised.

A sound from the doorway alerted her to the arrival of her mother and grandfather.

Lia's mom came rushing over to the bed, talking so fast and crying that Lia could not begin to understand what she said, but the words made Kaylee smile as she was touched with reverent affection by her grandmother.

Lia's grandfather still stood in the doorway, an expression on his face that Lia had never seen before. His stark angles were lined with grief and his eyes filled with it. He turned to her and she could see a sheen of tears.

"Rosalia, I…" He stopped, his voice choking to a halt. "I am sorry."

"Grandfather would you like to hug me before I go to sleep?" Kaylee asked from the bed in a voice faint with drug induced sleepiness.

He literally stumbled across the room and bent over the hospital bed with none of his usual elegant grace. He hugged Kaylee for a very long time telling her how much he loved her and how glad he was that she was all right.

When he was done, the nurse came in and suggested the visitors leave so Kaylee could sleep off the effects of the anesthesia. Lia wanted to sit with her daughter, but her grandfather asked her if he could speak to her.

She followed the others out of the room, feeling like she could face her grandfather and a roomful of more like him now that she *knew* her daughter was going to be okay.

"Rosalia, if we could have a moment of privacy?"

She'd never heard her grandfather sound diffident before and she didn't know how to respond to it.

"Anything you need to say to my wife you can say in front of me." Damian's instant defense and protective posture shouldn't have surprised her after what he had said in the courtyard, but it did.

The old man sighed heavily, but nodded. *"Eh, bien."* He put his hand out beseechingly toward her. "I am sorry, more sorry than I can say that I threatened you with your daughter's safety. In my mind it was all a power game. Like chess, where strategy was all that mattered. Our little Kaylee did not look sick. I could not think of her as sick. It was not until I saw her in that bed that I realized what I had truly done."

The passionately repentant speech shocked her into absolute silence.

A tear trickled down one weathered cheek. "I will understand if you can never find it in your heart to forgive me, but please believe. I never would have let her go without treatment. If you had refused to marry Damian, I would have found a way to provide it."

She wanted to believe that, if only because she loved the old man and couldn't stand the thought her daughter meant so little to him.

"I wanted you to be happy, *niña,* and for my sins, forcing you into the bargain with Damian was the only way I believed I could ensure your happiness."

"You're so sure I'll be happy with Damian?"

"I know it." A little of her grandfather's arrogance returned, but it was muted by the grief still mantling him like a dark and heavy cloak. "I groomed him for you from the day we met. I knew he would make you a good husband. I refused to let you go home to see that Tobias Kennedy."

"You didn't know about him."

"Of course, I did. You spent all your time with him the week after the funeral. Your mother was lost in her grief and she didn't see it, but I knew you had to be gotten away from the young man."

"He was a good man."

"Yes, but he was not the right man for you. He was too weak to care for you properly."

"Are you saying that you insisted we move to Spain and held me there as a virtual prisoner because you planned to marry me off to your protégé when I reached age?" It was so Machiavellian, it was unbelievable.

"*Sí*. And if I had not messed up somewhere along the way, all would have been well. Damian was attracted to you from the start, but you did not notice him. I thought you were still grieving your father. I did not realize you had been staying in contact with the American boy until after you eloped."

"What is this, what are you talking about?" Lia's mother demanded, her body tensed with distress.

Lia looked from her mother to her grandfather, who seemed to have aged twenty years over the past few minutes. Several things settled inside of her. She loved them both despite her mother's tendency to go through life in a fog that blunted her awareness of her family's needs and her grandfather's attempts toward manipulation.

"You pushed me right into his arms."

"I realized this. When it was too late."

"Using my fear for Kaylee to fix what *you* thought was a problem was wrong."

"I know and I am sorry." She'd never heard her grandfather use those words in all her life and now he'd said it three times in only a few minutes.

The genuineness of his repentance was unquestionable, but it did not erase all the pain from Lia's heart. "You hurt me."

"I have done little else since you were fifteen, but never once have I wanted that outcome. I see now that what you needed, I did not give. If I had, perhaps many things would have been different."

"Maybe," she conceded, though she didn't see the use in dwelling on that now.

Nothing could undo what had been done. She could not go back and undo her marriage to Toby even if she wanted to. And she didn't. Kaylee was worth all the pain Lia had experienced during and after her marriage.

But any relationship she had with her grandfather from this point forward had to be based on *mutual* respect. "If you want us in your life, you have to stop trying to orchestrate ours."

Grandfather nodded, frowning. "Damian has already made that very clear."

"I want to understand," her mother demanded again.

"I'll leave the telling to Grandfather, but it's going to be okay, Mama." She wasn't sure that was true, but Lia could not burden her mother with knowledge of her failure.

If her and Damian's marriage didn't work, it wouldn't be Grandfather's fault. And it wasn't his fault that marriage to Toby had brought so much pain to her. Maybe it was time she stopped blaming him for things that could not have been changed.

"I love you, Mama." She turned toward her grandfather. "I love you, too."

"Even after all this?"

"Even after. Love is like that." And only love could make the marriage between her and Damian work.

She saw that now, but that was a problem the two of them would have to work out.

Three days later, Damian and Lia returned to their apartment after leaving a quietly sleeping Kaylee at the hospital for her last overnight there. Damian suggested sharing the spa bath and she willingly agreed. They had been married for almost three weeks and the intimacy they shared continued to get better and better, making her believe maybe, just maybe, her marriage could work after all.

Damian settled her against him in the hot, bubbling water.

"You told me you were willing to try to achieve full intercourse on the day we agreed our marriage vows were binding. Did you mean that?" he asked, shattering the peace surrounding her like a pane of glass hit with a wrecking ball.

She gasped and tried to talk, but only unintelligible sounds came out of her mouth.

"I ask because there is a treatment."

She stared at him, still incapable of speech.

"For vaginismus," he clarified in her silence.

Memories she would rather forget surfaced. She wouldn't exactly call it a treatment. "My doctor told me."

"Then why have you not tried it?"

"Don't you think I did?" She'd tried so hard, but she'd never been able to overcome her body's reaction to the threat of intercourse. "It didn't work, I couldn't make my body relax."

"Maybe the doctor started with dilators that were too big."

"Dilators?"

"The treatment."

"What are you talking about?"

"You said your doctor told you about the treatment."

"My doctor said that vaginismus was the result of a subliminal desire on my part to withhold myself from Toby, that I was afraid of intimacy."

"He said what?"

"That if I loved Toby enough, my body would relax and let him enter me."

"That is ridiculous."

"It's what both the doctor and Toby believed, but I *did* love Toby. Maybe it wasn't the passionate and overwhelming feeling I…um, well anyway, it was real and I could still never control the spasms."

"Of course not. They are involuntary contractions of your vaginal muscles. No voluntary contraction could be nearly as complete. *It was not and is not your fault, do you hear me, querida?*"

He sounded fierce enough she'd have to be deaf not to have. "Yes, but the doctor said—"

"This doctor was an idiot."

He had been the same one to dismiss the hole in Kaylee's heart as an unimportant anomaly in test results, so she had to agree with Damian.

"Um…what are dilators?"

"The most widely accepted treatment for the spasms."

She felt embarrassed now that she had never even looked into treatment, but then until Damian, she'd had no reason to want to reclaim that aspect of her femininity. "You shouldn't know more about this than I do."

"Why do I?"

"I believed my doctor."

"Didn't you ever go for a second opinion, visit a specialist?"

"No."

"But the information I found is readily available on the Internet, and the one book I picked up was at the local bookstore. I did not even have to order it."

"What did the book say?"

"That the involuntary contraction is usually linked to sexual trauma in your past, but not necessarily rape."

"My wedding night…" she breathed. His brows rose in question, but she shook her head. She could tell him later. "You think residual fear from the trauma causes my spasms."

"It is possible. Your grandfather told me that you almost died giving birth to Kaylee. This too could have contributed."

After a long, painful labor, the placenta had torn and she still did her best to block the memory of the frantic pain-filled minutes that followed. She had no problem believing the experience impacted her ability to make love, but that didn't change her circumstances.

"Whether my doctor was right and I didn't want intimacy with Toby, or you are right about some subconscious fear causing the spasms, the problem is still inside my head and it's up to me to fix it."

"You are wrong, *mi mujer.*"

"But you just said—"

"That a trauma probably triggered it, but the treatment is not psychological. It is *physiological.* At least according to the vast majority of specialists in this area."

"You've done a lot of research."

"*Sí,* but you have not."

"After Toby died, I was sure I never wanted to be intimate with a man again."

He slid his hand across her breast, taunting her nipple with his fingers in the hot water. "And now?"

"I love intimacy with you," she said, stifling a groan of pleasure at the contact.

He turned her until they were looking at each other and her thighs were straddling his. "Tell me about your wedding night."

It was hard to concentrate on anything but Damian when the feel of his thighs against hers dominated her senses and his perfectly shaped body filled her vision.

She traced the brown disk of his nipple. "I was...very *intact* on my wedding night." It was getting easier to talk about this kind of thing with Damian. He knew as much about her body as she did, maybe more in some areas. She'd certainly never known she was capable of the pleasure he gave her. "It felt like Toby was ripping my body in two when we made love the first time. The second time wasn't much better. It still hurt, only he didn't have to try so hard to...you know. The next morning when he wanted to make love again, I cried and begged him not to."

"Did he rape you?" Damian looked ready to kill.

"No. I told you I'd never been raped, but he was a virgin, too, and he didn't always know how to touch me without hurting me, but he would never have forced himself on me. I let him try again a couple of nights later, but that was the first time my body rejected him. Neither one of us knew what to do and we were both too embarrassed to ask anyone about it, but after six months without sex, he told me I had to ask my doctor."

"And your doctor told you it was all in your head."

"He suggested I drink a glass of wine before trying to make love. It didn't help, but Toby tried more frequently and managed penetration a few times."

Damian's frown was ferocious, but his voice was mild when he spoke. "Are you still afraid of being hurt?"

Remembering her reaction to his finger, she nodded. "I must be. I don't want to be. I *know* you wouldn't hurt me, but Toby and I never had what you would call a successful attempt at lovemaking. And after Kaylee was born, the spasms happened every time we tried to make love. I told him he could try to force it a few times, but it didn't work. We both ended up in tears and hurting."

Damian cupped her face with gentle, wet hands. "And even after that your doctor told you it was all your fault?"

"He thought I had some deep-seated need to have control in the relationship. Toby thought I didn't love him enough. He loved me, but he couldn't stay in a marriage without sex."

"He could have," Damian ground out, dropping his hands to her hips and pulling her more intimately against him. "He chose not to."

"It amounts to the same thing." She could feel his hard flesh right against the heart of her. She couldn't help squirming against him and increasing the friction.

The movement made them both groan.

"Perhaps, but his choice left you with a mistaken impression of what you had to offer in a marriage."

"I didn't know what it could offer me, either. I thought getting married again would end up putting me through the hell I knew with Toby. Until you touched me, I didn't know what it meant to really want someone."

He liked hearing that. The forgivably smug expression on his face said so. "Do you want to hear about the dilators?"

"Yes."

His dark gaze caught hers and held it captive. "Short, narrow cylinders are placed here." He touched her intimately. "They start smaller than a Q-tip and are replaced in graduated sizes until the muscles have been stretched enough to accept intercourse."

Thinking of the size of his erection, she frowned with chagrin and opened her eyes. "It would take a year to get me ready to receive you."

He laughed, the sound masculine and warm. "No, it will not. Once you reach a certain point of dilation, your body will stretch to accommodate me without pain."

She didn't know if she could stand having a doctor administer the treatment. She knew it would require such a thing for her to become whole, but it was something so intimate to have done in a doctor's office. Her memories of her visits to the doctor were not appreciably better than those of her times of intimacy with Toby.

"How many visits to the doctor would it take?" she asked, trying not to look as repelled by the idea as she felt.

His expression said he wasn't fooled. "You do not like the idea of having a doctor touching you so intimately?"

"You asked me if I was willing to try to achieve full intercourse, the answer is yes," she said instead of answering his most recent question.

He was not fooled by her evasion tactics and his dark, knowing eyes said so. "Nothing dictates only a doctor may administer the dilators."

"Who else could do it?" A nurse? She wasn't sure that would be any better.

"Me."

"*You?*" she squeaked, shock coursing through her at the idea.

"*Sí, querida.* Me."

"But…"

"I would not hurt you."

"*I know,* but…" Her voice trailed off because she wasn't sure what to say.

She wanted to try and not just because she'd made a promise. If she could have a complete sexual relationship with Damian, she wanted it. Another woman might feel differently, but the idea of her lover witnessing her body's refusal to function sexually was more palatable than a stranger doing so, even if he or she was a doctor.

"Let me do it, Lia." His voice compelled her as did the expression in his dark eyes.

"Do you really think it will work?" Hope burned hot and deep inside her.

"According to what I have read, the procedure is almost always successful in making sexual intimacy possible. Sometimes, muscle relaxers are necessary and it could take more than one time to achieve our goal, but that is hardly a problem. We have the rest of our lives together, *mi esposa.*"

"How will you go about it?" she asked, giving her tacit agreement to trying. "I mean do you just stick it in?"

"When it comes to touching you here…" His finger brushed along her feminine heart. "I will never *just stick* anything in. I will touch you until you are lubricated then slide the first one in. Some of the articles I read said you should leave each dilator in for ten minutes, others until you feel ready for the next size, but the author of the book thought five minutes for each graduation would be sufficient."

"What do you think?"

"That we should only do what feels right and good to you. We are not in a doctor's office. We can take as long as we want to and I have the advantage of knowing I can arouse you. I believe your body will adjust to the dilators faster if you are sexually excited."

That made sense, but it was all so unbelievable. Not only the procedure itself, but the fact he had made the effort to research it all and come up with a solution. "When do you want to do it?"

"I will get a set of dilators and then we will see. Kaylee's needs are paramount right now."

"You are an amazing man, did you know that?"

His slashing grin made her heart flip over. "I am glad you think so because I believe you are the bravest woman I have ever known."

She shook her head, but he kissed any denial from her lips and then showed her once again that the shades of intimacy in marriage were varied and beautiful.

They spent five days at the apartment, spending a good part of each one in the company of Lia's mother and grandfather. Once the doctor gave Kaylee the okay, they flew to New York in Damian's private plane. When they arrived, she was delighted to discover he owned a house upstate.

He told her it was only a ninety-minute train ride into the city.

"You're gone commuting three hours a day?" she asked, aghast.

"I have an apartment in the city as well. I used to stay there five days a week, but I am concentrating on doing more of my business from my office here now."

"I'm glad."

He smiled. "You do not want me gone five days a week?" he teased.

"Kaylee and I would just follow you," she teased right back, growing more confident with him daily. "I hope your office in New York is big."

"It is large and it has a very comfortable sofa."

"For sitting?"

"Among other things."

She grabbed his silk tie and pulled him toward her. "Has it had a lot of that kind of use?" she asked only half jokingly.

His dark eyes mocked her. "What *use* would that be, *querida?*"

"You know what I mean, Don Damian Marquez."

"Sleeping?" he asked innocently.

She dropped his tie and spun on her heel, but he grabbed her from behind and brought her back around to face him with an implacable hold.

All humor had drained from his expression. "No, *querida*. It has not. You need not concern yourself with such worries regarding my office or our home. Our bed here is untouched. Any exciting moments of an intimate nature that occur in my office will be with you and you alone. As my wife, you are the only woman that exists for me anymore."

She let her body melt against him and smiled. She thought she would like to be the only woman who existed for him because he couldn't imagine wanting anyone else, but his declaration had still been pretty special. "You know exactly the right thing to say."

Soon his warm, firm mouth sent all other thoughts to the very darkest recesses of her mind.

He made no move to try the dilators for the next week and she was hesitant to ask why. Maybe he hadn't gotten any yet, but then again maybe he wasn't looking forward to having to do what was basically a medical procedure on her. He hadn't sounded like he minded doing it, though. In fact, he'd sounded pretty eager and very understanding.

So, maybe he was waiting for her to say something. She vacillated over what to do for two more days before deciding the wait was worse than knowing, even if he said he would prefer she go to a doctor for the treatment.

Damian walked into the bedroom he shared with Lia, anticipating that moment when he would slide between the sheets and take his wife in his arms. It felt so right, this cuddling they did before and during sleep. Even on the rare occasions they went to sleep without arousing each other, it felt better than anything he had ever known.

He felt *intimate* with his wife and no way was he ever letting her walk out on their marriage.

"Damian…" Her voice called out softly in the darkness and he stopped undressing.

He turned toward the bed, his slacks undone and his shirt discarded. *"Que?"*

"I was wondering…" Her voice ended abruptly, as if she couldn't make the next words come out.

"What is it?"

The lamp on her nightstand clicked on, revealing her beautiful form covered in the sexiest bit of nothing he'd ever seen. His heart jump-started and he experienced an immediate reaction that left him ready for things she'd probably never even considered.

The lingerie purchase.

He had wondered when he would get to see it. His only complaint now was that half of her was covered by the sheet.

"You look beautiful."

"Thank you."

"Is this what you wanted to discuss? If so, we can both agree you have impeccable taste in nightwear."

She laughed softly, her amber eyes glinting with desire and something more. Nervousness. Then, she took a deep breath, as if preparing to plunge into deep waters. "Have you had a chance to get the dilators?"

"I had them the day after we discussed it."

"Then why…"

"Why have I done nothing about it?" he asked when it appeared she was not going to finish her question.

"Yes."

"The past days, you have been very concerned for Kaylee, no?"

"Yes, I have."

"And this has made you tense."

She grimaced. "Yes, it has."

"It is best for you to be relaxed and worry-free the first time we attempt dilation. I refuse to give you another negative sexual experience." In fact, he would do his utmost to stop her from having one ever again.

"How could you?" she asked, sounding genuinely puzzled. "There is nothing negative about the way you touch me. It's all so perfect."

She was the perfect one. Perfect for him. "I am glad you find it so."

"I'm not worried about Kaylee anymore," she said with quiet hesitation. "I mean…the surgeon said her heart beats like there was never a hole in it. And… um…she's sleeping peacefully in her bedroom *now.*"

A bedroom that was only across the hall from theirs so the little girl could easily find them if she woke nervous in the night. However the walls in the house had been built almost soundproof and now he appreciated that feature very much. Once their bedroom door was shut, they would be isolated in their own private world.

"Are you saying you want to try tonight?" he asked.

Her cheeks turned rose red, but she nodded with absolute assurance. "Yes."

Want and need jolted through him at her acquiescence and he finished undressing in record time. She watched him with intent fascination, her attention never straying from him and what he was doing.

He walked to the bed, his eyes locked with hers, his already excited flesh tight and full with his need. Her gaze flicked down to it and then up again, her pupils dilated. When he reached her, he put one knee beside her on the bed. She flinched slightly, but did not pull away.

He cupped her cheek. "You are nervous."

"And excited."

Both were to be expected. However, he would have to show her that she had no reason to be nervous of him and every excuse for excitement. "Tonight we replace your first wedding night with a new one full of pleasure not pain."

CHAPTER TEN

"YOU already did that." She smiled tremulously at him. "On our wedding night. You held me after I refused you. That was really special to me. I hadn't been held in so long and had never felt so safe."

His eyes closed and he fought unfamiliar emotion. "Lia…"

Her lips met his, the kiss taking him by surprise, but not for long. He devoured her lips, demanding absolute surrender because it had to be so. She seemed to understand and gave him everything his kiss claimed of her.

They were both shaking when he pulled away.

She whimpered, her nipples rigid points against the sheer lace of her teddy and his sex throbbed in response to the evidence of her need.

"I will get the dilators."

She nodded, total trust burning at him from her golden eyes.

Before he came down beside her again, he pulled the blankets and top sheet off the bed, revealing her entire body to his heated gaze.

The basque was scandalous in its miniscule proportions, the lace v-ing between her legs barely covering the silky curls that hid her secrets and the cut on the hips so high, it was almost to her waist.

"Very nice," he rasped, shocked by how hard it was to get words out past his tight throat.

"Thank you," she practically purred, stretching with a wantonness she never would have shown before the many passionate sessions of lovemaking in their marriage.

He loved the show of confidence, and like everything else about her, it increased his primitive desire to connect at the most fundamental level.

She put her arms out to him, an invitation as old as time and as beautiful as eternity. "Make love to me, Damian."

That was all it took for him to move. He covered her in a rush of need, pressing his lips against hers which were parted invitingly and kissed her with every bit of seductive skill at his disposal. He wanted her aching for him, pulsing with a craving only he could fill. The hunger in her lips easily matched his own and she was writhing in restless abandon under him almost immediately.

The hard tips of her breasts pressed against his chest, instilling a hunger that demanded immediate fulfillment. He took precious seconds divesting her of her sexy nightwear. He then went on a tasting expedition down the delicate column of her throat, over the flushed skin of her chest, to the soft, resilient flesh of her generous curves. He usually made a feast of them, but right now he wanted…needed…had to have…a tasting of her distended peaks.

He closed his mouth over one and exerted an immediate, gentle suction. Her body jerked as if struck with an electric jolt and he increased the pull of his mouth until she arched toward him, panting out her need.

"Damian…" His name was a long, drawn-out moan of desire.

No music had ever sounded sweeter, or lovelier to his ears. He adored her instant response to his slightest touch. She was the most amazing lover he'd ever known. Other women might have been more knowledgeable about the practiced technique that stirred a man's senses, but none of them had made him tremble with need. Only Lia could do that.

He played with her creamy, soft flesh, kneading her with fingers that shook, tasting her with his mouth, and nipping at her with careful provocation. Soon, not only her back was arched toward him in a silent demand for more, but her pelvis was tilting up toward him with the same fierce abandon.

It was what he had been waiting for. He slipped his hand between her legs and slid the first dilator inside her.

She made a startled sound and went stiff.

"Are you all right, *querida?*"

Lia didn't know how to answer Damian. "It doesn't hurt." It just felt alien, but then so had his finger on the few occasions he had managed to caress her inner flesh before it closed up.

"Bueno." He put his mouth on her breast again, his suction erotically intense and even the feeling of her body tightening around the small cylinder could not mute the pure pleasure he gave her.

But she wasn't sure if she was supposed to react this way to the dilator, so she said, "I'm tightening up."

"Does it hurt?"

"No."

"Then do not worry about it." His voice was rich with passion and approval, making it easy to do as he said.

He came up over her, aligning their bodies in warm intimacy and kissed her, his scent and the textures of his skin dominating her senses. She moaned and touched him everywhere she could reach, wanting to torment him with as much pleasure as he gave her. It seemed to be working because he made dark sounds of masculine need deep in his throat and moved against her with primitive force.

She loved that he did not withhold his passion from her, but that she also knew beyond a doubt she could trust him not to press for more than her body could give. He'd proven it to her over and over again in their non-consummated lovemaking.

"I think I could handle the next one," she panted seconds later as she felt pulsing sensations in her feminine core that had nothing to do with pain or fear.

He didn't say anything, but his hand went between her thighs and with sensual, but gentle mastery, he made the change. He never stopped kissing and touching her so she was ready for the next graduation very soon thereafter.

This time her body resisted, but her need was greater than her fear of failure and she begged, "Please, don't stop. There's no pain. I promise."

It took all Damian's control not to explode right there. She was so beautiful in her passion. Her dark, silky hair was spread across the pillow, her eyes wild with desire, and her body flushed from his lovemaking.

"I will not stop, *mi esposa preciosa.*" This was too important to both of them.

But if he did not do something to assuage his primal need to claim her body, he was going to lose control and that was not something either of them could afford to risk.

He began kissing his way down her body, exploring the sexy indentation of her belly button in minute detail with his tongue. When he moved lower, he parted her with his fingers, opening her to the possession of his mouth. She moaned and writhed and pulled at his hair when he kissed her between the legs, arching toward his mouth.

He concentrated on her sweetest spot, hungry for the sounds she made when she convulsed with pleasure. She shuddered with release as he changed the dilators once again, her silky wetness sweet against his tongue.

The succession up to the finger size dilator went by more quickly than he had anticipated, the residual satiation from her completion relaxing her body for easy penetration. Her initial fear had melted away completely and she didn't even flinch when he put the larger cylinder inside her opening.

It was only a matter of seconds before she panted that she was ready for the next one.

He touched her tentatively, running his finger along the slick and swollen tissue. "Now we go to my finger, okay?"

She nodded, her eyes filled with a mixture of excitement and renewed fear, but it was obvious her desire was much bigger than her worry. He moved up to kiss her mouth while he carefully pulled the dilator out and then slipped his finger inside.

Wet silk closed around him with such enticement his

sex ached in response. He wanted her so much, but this had to be perfect for her.

She deserved it.

He pleasured her with his finger, making this dilation a much more active step.

She moaned and writhed some more and when he went to slide a second finger in with the first, she didn't tense up at all. "That feels so good, Damian. Ahhhh…" Her voice cracked and went silent as he touched her the way he had wanted to since their wedding night.

However, she was tight and it took several minutes of gentle coaxing before her body relaxed around his fingers. Once it did, he moved them in and out with the same rhythm he would use to join their bodies.

She loved it, pushing herself toward his hand, taking him in as far as he would go. She pulled her mouth from his and panted, her face flushed with uncontrolled desire. "I'm ready for you, Damian, I know I am."

He looked into her golden eyes, darkened with wanting, the emotion burning enough to send him over the edge even without the thought of being inside her.

"Are you certain?" he asked. "There is a big jump from my fingers to me."

"You said there would come a time when my body would stretch to accommodate you. I think that time is now." She spread her legs wider under him, bringing her knees up to make room for him in her secret place.

He had passed hot to incendiary two dilation levels ago and did not begin to have the willpower or even the desire to continue arguing with her.

She tilted her pelvis upward in blatant invitation. "Make me yours."

"You have always been mine. Make no mistake, but now I join our bodies as intimately as two bodies can be."

He pushed inside. It was tight and he couldn't get much more than the tip of his erect flesh in at first, but he rocked gently against her and she strained upward.

"It's working!" The elation in her voice made his eyes sting and he buried his face in the fragrant hair lying against her neck.

He'd never experienced anything so profound in all his life.

Lia could not believe the sensation of fullness without pain she was experiencing. She'd never known anything like it. It was *nothing* like her disastrous wedding night. Damian was gentle and coaxing, not taking her body like a marauding invader, but enticing her to accept him, all of him.

And she wanted to. She wanted to so much! It felt beyond good. It felt wonderful.

She strained upward, rocking her own pelvis until the muscles inside her body gave and Damian pushed forward to fill her completely, stretching her inside to pleasure a step away from pain. But it was not pain and she could have cried at the beauty of it.

He started to move on her with a cadence she knew well. Only before, when he'd used it, he had not been inside her body like he was now. It felt very, very different this time. She moved with him and experienced the shattering sensations in the very core of her being.

Soon his breathing was hard and so was hers.

"Yes, Damian. Darling, yes!"

"*Querida,* you feel so perfect. I want—" He bit off

his words and she guessed he wanted to be rougher, but he'd promised gentleness from the very beginning.

"Don't hold back, *please*. You aren't hurting me. *I want to feel everything with you inside me.*"

Her words seemed to drive him wild because he started to plunge into her with powerful thrusts. Each stroke hit some secret spot inside of her body that made her shudder with pleasure over and over again. The sensation grew more and more devastating until she splintered apart, explosions going off inside her with the power of a nuclear reactor in meltdown.

Her body contracted around his hardness and she bowed up against him with more strength than she knew she had, lifting them both off the bed.

"*Sí, querida*. Give yourself to the pleasure of our joined bodies." He kept loving her and incredibly, it happened again, stronger than the first time.

He had taught her that her body was capable of prolonged pleasure, but even in his arms, she had never known anything like this. It was indescribably sweet and devastatingly powerful, both too much and not enough. She wanted to beg him to stop, but she would die if he didn't continue. The only sounds she could force out of her tight throat were unintelligible groans anyway.

And he didn't stop, didn't even slow down. How could any person maintain such powerful action for so long? More tension built low in her belly and this time she was determined not to go through the cataclysmic explosion alone. She wrapped her legs around his hips, her arms around his neck, and then stretched up so she could take his nipple into her mouth.

She bit him gently and caressed him with her tongue. When she started sucking, he went rigid and then flooded her with pulsing heat while his shout rang in her ears.

Her body convulsed again, this time sharing the experience so completely with him that she felt like they were one person, their bodies joined on a much more profound level than the mere physical. She didn't faint, but she was light-headed and it was all she could do to keep her arms wrapped around him.

They felt like overcooked spaghetti noodles.

He went to pull away, but she held him to her, discovering energy she didn't know she had. "Please, it's wonderful. So special. Don't leave me."

"I am too heavy."

She clung. "No. You aren't."

"I am, but I too enjoy the closeness and have no wish to move." His smile was so gentle, she could be forgiven for believing it held more than simple physical satiation.

He kissed her.

Moisture burned her eyes, but she refused to let it spill over. She would not spoil this moment, even with happy tears.

His lips slid to her temple and he placed a kiss there that was no less than a benediction to her soul.

"Oh, Damian."

Holding their bodies as tightly together as possible, in one deft move he reversed positions and she was on top of him. He was still inside of her.

She looked down into his face, the quiet approval she saw there touching her more deeply than she'd ever allowed another human being to touch her. "I love you,

Damian. So very much. Thank you for helping me to be a real woman."

His expression turned fierce. "You have always been a real woman. *Thank you* for sharing your body with me."

He hadn't responded to her avowal of love, but she hadn't expected him to. He might not love her, but he'd given her more than Toby ever had, or anyone else who said they loved her had, in her whole life.

He pulled her mouth to his for a long, lingering kiss and then caressed her back with soft, soothing strokes until she fell asleep.

She woke up with him making love to her sometime in the night and cried with joy when her body accepted him without having to use the dilators.

The next day, Lia bubbled with joy, the only cloud on her horizon the fact her husband did not love her. But he wanted to be married to her and that counted for a lot. He also desired her and enjoyed her company. He was committed to her well-being and that of her daughter. She wasn't sure even love would carry with it anything more than what he so generously gave.

He didn't trust love and she could understand why, but one day, he would change his mind. She would show him that loving her was not wrong or risky.

He was working in his study when unexpected visitors arrived. Toby's parents.

The housekeeper showed the elderly couple into the sunroom where Lia and Kaylee worked on an art project together. Kaylee's squeal of delight brought Lia's head up with a quick jerk and then a smile of welcome spread across her own features.

She jumped up along with Kaylee and they both rushed across the room to hug the tiny woman and big barrel of a man that reminded Lia so much of her late husband.

"Edna, Bruce…this is a wonderful surprise!"

"We thought we'd give you a little while to get used to being married again before showing up on your doorstep, but I finally couldn't wait to see my baby girl." Edna hugged Kaylee close. "The phone just wasn't enough."

Guilt assailed Lia. She should have had her former in-laws flown to Seattle to be there during Kaylee's procedure. "I didn't think of arranging for you to come. I should have."

Bruce shook his head. "No need to worry about us, young lady. You've had plenty on your plate lately."

But she should have worried. She was so used to living on a tight budget, her new circumstances had not sunk into her thought processes yet. Three months ago, paying for the plane tickets for Kaylee's grandparents to come visit would have been as impossible as financing the little girl's surgery.

She shook her head. "I can't dismiss my thoughtlessness so easily. I am sorry."

"You kept us up on the news by phone," Bruce reminded her.

"But a hug is worth a thousand phone calls," Edna said, making Kaylee giggle as she tickled the little girl.

Lia's smile was forced as she invited them to take a seat. She loved these two people and no matter what they said, she'd let them down.

Bruce and Edna took up the chairs on either side of Kaylee at the table covered with art supplies.

"I'll get something for you two to drink." Lia turned to do just that and stopped abruptly at the sight of her frowning husband standing in the doorway.

"I was told we have visitors."

"Grandpa and Grandma came to see me, Papa!" Kaylee yelled excitedly from the other side of the room, practically bouncing in her chair.

Bruce flinched at the word Papa and Edna's smile dimmed a little, but they both rose to meet Damian and shake his hand.

"We owe you a debt of gratitude," Bruce said, his emotions close to the surface. "Lia told us that you made it possible for her to pay for Kaylee's procedure."

Nothing could be read in Damian's expression, but he shook the older man's hand. "Kaylee and Lia are my family now. Rest assured, I will always look out for their needs."

Bruce's smile was tinged with sadness. "Yes."

Lia wished she knew what to say to ease the obvious burden of pain in the man who had been her only real father figure since the death of her own at age fifteen. But everything she considered saying would sound disloyal to Damian. Conflicting love and loyalty twisted her insides just as her hands twisted together in front of her.

Damian noticed and reached out to gently disentangle them, folding his big hand around one of hers. His eyes asked if she was all right and she tried to reassure him with her own, but guilt and sadness weighed on her heart.

He narrowed his eyes and then turned to Bruce and

Edna. "I owe you and your son an even greater debt, however. Tobias Kennedy fathered my precious step-daughter. I am honored to be Kaylee's papa, but your son will always be her father. Since his death, you have taken care of Lia and Kaylee as only family can. For that, I am forever in your debt."

"Nonsense," Bruce blustered, but Edna's eyes filled with tears and she choked trying to get words out.

"You are very important people to both my wife and my daughter and I hope you will see your way to spending a great deal of time with us here in New York."

"We would like nothing better," Edna said, obvious tears in her eyes.

Lia couldn't help it. Her own eyes filled with tears and she gave Bruce and Edna a watery smile. "Is it any wonder I love him so much?"

"You've found yourself another good man," Bruce said. He met Damian's gaze square on. "We were both worried about Lia marrying again. She deserved the best and I'm glad to see she's gotten it."

Damian's thanks was obviously sincere.

The rest of the visit went smoothly and the elderly couple was convinced to transfer their belongings from a nearby hotel to Damian's home for the remainder of their stay.

"You were tense when I first arrived in the sunroom this afternoon." Damian spoke from where he sat on the bed removing his shoes.

As always, when her husband began undressing, Lia's brain had a hard time focusing on anything else. "I was?" she asked absently.

"You looked unhappy."

And he sounded bothered by that fact.

She forced herself to remember. "I felt guilty. I could have made sure they were there when Kaylee had her procedure, but I didn't even think of it. They offered to sell their house to pay for the surgery we all thought she needed, but it wouldn't have been enough money. Yet they were willing to make the sacrifice and I let them down, even if they don't see it that way."

"I am sorry. I should have considered this as well."

"You can't think of everything."

"I usually do, but if you want the truth, I did not like the thought of your former husband's family having a claim on you."

"But you were so kind to them."

He continued undressing, the sight of his muscular chest coming into view doing things to her breathing. "Your loyalty to me came first and I saw this. It was enough."

"You are so special."

His expression wasn't one she recognized. Sometimes she wished she could read her husband's complex mind.

He stood up and unzipped his pants. "They are older than I expected."

She had already changed into a satin robe and she busied herself hanging up the dress she'd worn for dinner. "They had Toby late in life. He was an unexpected blessing after years of trying and finally giving up on having children."

"It must have been very hard for them when he was killed."

She sighed and turned to face Damian again, her mouth going dry at the sight of his naked body. "I-it was," she stuttered out, having to concentrate on what had been said before she could speak. "They latched on to Kaylee and me, but they supported us as well. I owe them a lot and I really appreciate you being so sensitive to them."

"I am not the most sensitive of men, *querida,* but family is family."

She begged to differ on the sensitivity part, but she just smiled. "Well, I'm glad you don't mind them being a part of our life. They're very special to me."

"They were bothered that Kaylee calls me Papa."

"That's to be expected, but I think they were ultimately okay with it. You did a tremendous job of setting their minds at rest."

"And you, are you ultimately okay with me being her Papa?"

How could he even need to ask that? "I'm more than okay with it. I'm grateful she has a daddy again. I'm thrilled that man is you. I love you, Damian." The words got easier to say even though he never said them back.

He sat down on the side of the bed again. "Gratitude is not love."

She settled into his lap and looped her arms around his neck. "No, it's not, but then what I feel for you is so much bigger than gratitude. I passionately want you. I adore spending time with you. You make me feel like a complete woman, even when we're just together like we were in the sunroom this afternoon. I love you, Damian. Believe me."

He picked her up and carried her to the en suite. "Bathe with me."

"Yes."

But it bothered her a little he had not said he believed her. Did he really think she could mistake gratitude for love?

He made a production out of removing her silky bathrobe while the water ran to fill the spa bath. Scooping her up, he stepped into the hot water and sat down with her in his lap once again.

"I love you," she whispered over and over again as he kissed her neck, along her collarbone, her shoulders and the tops of her breasts.

She wanted to imprint the words on his soul.

Finally his lips swallowed her continued whispered avowals and within minutes they were straining together in the bubbling water. She touched his hard length and he shuddered.

Smiling with feminine delight, she stroked him into complete readiness. Willingly she allowed her legs to be pressed apart and his hand to trespass on her most feminine place. When she felt her body tighten around his finger, she refused to accept it was happening at first. But no amount of denial could stop the truth from crashing through her like a marauding stampede of cattle, trampling her heart in their wake.

A cry of despair rose up, but he cut that off with his lips, too, giving her a hard, possessive kiss. "Hold that thought, *mi esposa*."

He climbed out of the bathtub and walked sleek and naked back into the bedroom. He returned seconds later with a small, familiar plastic case.

She stared at the case with a mixture of despair and

bitter knowledge. "You can't want to go through this every time we make love," she wailed.

He stopped with his foot on the edge of the bath and looked down at her in all his naked glory. "Do you think it bothers me to kiss your breasts, to take their peaks into my mouth?"

"No."

"And yet, I do this every time we make love."

"It's not the same thing."

"Is it not?"

She opened her mouth to speak, but he overrode her.

"Who is to say what a man enjoys doing with his woman?"

He climbed into the tub and pulled her back into his arms. She tried to resist, but he would have none of it and she was no match for his strength. She ended up on his lap, his erection pressing against her hip.

The plastic case that produced such ambivalent feelings in her sat on the oversize spa's tile edge, right in her line of vision.

His hand trespassed the intimate heart of her again, his finger gently caressing her sweetest spot. "You are so soft here, so silky and it excites me to touch you."

Her breathing splintered. "Ye-es."

The knowing finger went lower and touched the flesh closed to him. "I love touching you here."

"I love it, too…" Her voice trailed off in breathless delight as he pleasured her with his hand.

"It matters not to me if the touch is to put a dilator in to stretch you so we can make love, or it is simply to run my fingers over your tempting feminine flesh. *I enjoy it all*. Would you deny me the right to touch you as I wish, in the ways that give me pleasure as well as pleasing you? Each touch excites me and fills me with satisfaction that you open yourself to me so completely."

She desperately wanted that to be true, but could it be?

The doubt must have reflected in her eyes because he growled in obvious displeasure at her disbelief and then kissed her in a way that dared her to deny him anything.

She didn't. She couldn't.

When he finally lifted his mouth, her lips pulsed with need for more. But she had to say, "There's still my sexual dysfunction."

His hand traced her breast in the water. "For me, you function perfectly sexually."

"But we have to use the dilators…"

"And that excites me."

He didn't look like he was kidding and she knew he would never lie to her. "It *excites* you to use them?"

Wasn't that a little kinky?

"It is something private and special between us. A thing I do for you that no one else can do. Preparing you to receive me in this way is as intimate as the act of love itself. Of course it makes me want you more."

If she tried to speak, she would choke on her emotion, so she kissed him, trying to infuse her lips with the huge love she felt for him and the overwhelming gratefulness to God that this man was her husband.

He took her through the dilation and then made love to her, all of it there in the hot waters of the spa. And the whole time, he praised her for her passion, told her how much he loved the way her flesh swelled around him, that he couldn't wait to be inside her and share the pleasure together.

When they did make love completely, it was every bit as earth-shattering as it had been before.

Damian worked in his study while his wife entertained her and Kaylee's guests. At least he was supposed to be working. He was thinking about her avowals of love instead.

She said the words often, as if she hoped that by repeating them he would accept them. She had to sense his reservations about the reality of her gift. For her love would indeed be a gift. A necessary gift. One he was not sure he could continue to live without.

If only he could be sure that it was love. She said often how much he had given her, implying she owed him some immeasurable debt of gratitude for each thing. He did not want gratitude masquerading as love. He needed the real thing.

Kaylee's grandparents stayed a week and left with the assurance that Damian would bring Lia and Kaylee to New Mexico for a visit very soon.

That night, Lia walked into her and Damian's bedroom to find a carved wooden heart sitting on her pillow. It was about four-by-six inches and the laced carving in the dark, polished wood looked both intricate and lovely.

She walked forward slowly, hope and love and fear, swirling together in a heady mixture inside her.

Could this mean what she so desperately wanted it to mean? Hearts meant love, didn't they? Romantic love. Man-woman, forever after love. Valentines and sentimental romance. Everything she wanted from him. She lifted the heart, enjoying the sensation of her fingertips against its smoothly polished sides.

This close up she could see the top was covered in tiny carved roses and rosebuds, intertwined by vines with delicate leaves. Only in the center, the roses seemed to fade away, leaving an opening in which the words, *Tu tienes mi Corazon* had been carved in a scrolling script.

Her eyes burned with moisture as her heart contracted. *You have my heart.* Did she? Could she? The possibility stole every other thought from her head.

Two strong arms came around her and she gasped.

He didn't say anything, but his hands covered her own. He lifted the lid from the heart. Inside, on a bed of rich red velvet was an assortment of dilators.

"Are you ready to make love to your husband?" he asked, his voice seducing her every bit as effectively as the proximity of his body.

She smiled, feeling feminine and strong, while hope beat a wild tattoo in her heart. "Yes, but I don't think we're going to need those." She indicated the dilators. They hadn't at all the past three nights.

"Can we use them anyway?"

She looked at him startled, her breath suspended in her chest.

He was saying something important here and it wasn't about wanting to make love with accoutrements.

He turned her around and cupped her face in his hands. "I love *you,* Lia."

The tears spilled over and he smiled, not in the least bothered by her emotional reaction.

"When I first met you, I wanted you. You were too

young, but I never forgot you and when your grandfather suggested a merger marriage, I was intrigued. When I saw you again, the desire you sparked in me almost sent me to my knees."

"Desire is not love."

His smile turned incredibly tender. "You told me you felt more for me than gratitude."

It almost sounded like a question and she had no hesitation in reassuring him. "I do. So much more. I can't deny my thankfulness for all that you have given me, but the greatest gift in our marriage to me has been yourself. I love you, completely."

"I also feel this love you speak of. I do desire you. More than any other woman in the world, but I feel so much more for you than mere physical need. Love is the only word that can describe the way my soul belongs to yours."

She had hoped. She had wanted. She had desperately needed this to be true, but one doubt remained.

"Even with my problem?" she asked with aching vulnerability she could not begin to hide.

"It is not a problem for me. *I love you.*" He pressed a soul caressing kiss to her more than willing lips. "This means I love your body and *everything* your body does."

He picked her up and carried her to the bed, laying her down so she faced him. Then he tugged the wooden heart from her hands and tipped it over, pouring the set of graduated cylinders on the comforter between them. "These represent your trust in me, our desire for each other and the will to bridge any gap to keep our marriage strong. To me, they are beautiful, just as you are beautiful because in a way, they are part of you, but they are part of me also."

"Yes." She understood and the understanding filled her with more joy than she'd ever known.

That joy was reflected in his amazing dark eyes. "I love you, *all of you,* for all time."

She looked at the small cylinders he'd used to help her reclaim her womanhood then into the eyes of her tycoon husband. She had married him looking for a way to save her daughter's life, but he had given her so much more. He had given her a new life of her own. "I love you, Damian, all of you, for all time," she repeated.

"I know." His hand curved possessively over the indentation of her waist. "It took me time to accept it, but I believe you now. What we have is nothing like what I have ever known and you are a woman unlike any other."

"It's not gratitude," she reiterated.

"*Sí.* No more than what I feel for you is mere lust. It is love, pure and strong."

More tears filled her eyes and she let them fall. Her heart was so full, she couldn't stop them. "I'm so glad."

"I also, *mi corazón.*"

He pulled her into his arms and she eagerly snuggled into him. "You are the very air that I breathe. I will never let you go."

She remembered how hard he had fought to keep their marriage viable from the start. "You've given me so much."

"You have given me more. You have given me a family again. To be Don Damian Marquez holds no importance beside the titles of husband and father. You have enriched my life beyond measure."

"Oh, Damian…" She kissed him, letting every bit of

emotion inside her flow freely from her heart to his. When she pulled back, they were both shaking. "I love you."

"Until the last breath in my body and then into eternity." His kiss sealed the vow.

Lia gently laid her tiny son in his crib. It was the same one his brother had used two years ago. She could not believe the changes in her life three years of marriage to Damian had wrought. She had a closer relationship with both her grandfather and mother. She also had three children and Damian loved them all with the same fierce, possessive tenderness he felt for her.

The box of dilators still resided on her dresser, dusted daily by their maid, but it had not been opened since before the birth of their first son. Damian refused to get rid of it, saying he wanted her to remember he would always be willing to bridge whatever gap might emerge in their marriage.

And he had, too, lovingly participating in parenthood as only a reformed workaholic tycoon could do.

"Is he sleeping?"

She turned and smiled, her heart catching as it always did at the sight of her gorgeous husband. "Yes."

"Then you are all mine?"

"Always."

He swept her into his arms and carried her through the connecting door to their bedroom. He made love to her whispering a litany of love and need that grew richer as time went on, but did not diminish.

He was her world and she was his and their love grew stronger with every passing year.

Neither one of them would ever take that love for granted, either, because they knew it was too much of a miracle.

A note to readers from Lucy: One in three women has a physiological sexual dysfunction, which means her body physically responds to lovemaking in a negative way. The most common of these dysfunctions is vulvadynia, but vaginismus is not nearly as rare as many medical doctors would like to believe, nor is it always the result of sexual trauma, although pain related to sexuality is the leading identifiable cause. I wrote this book for the tens of thousands of women who suffer in silence believing there is something wrong with *them*. Only one in ten will seek treatment and of those, less than thirty percent will be willing to undergo physiological treatment such as the dilation procedure for vaginismus. I hope that if you are one of the women suffering in silence, you will be silent no longer, but most of all that you will realize that it's not your fault—no more than it was Kaylee's fault in the story that she was born with a heart defect. She got her happy ending and I hope you get yours, too.

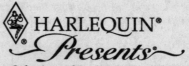

If you enjoyed what you just read,
then we've got an offer you can't resist!

Take 2 bestselling love stories FREE!

Plus get a FREE surprise gift!

Clip this page and mail it to Harlequin Reader Service®

IN U.S.A.
3010 Walden Ave.
P.O. Box 1867
Buffalo, N.Y. 14240-1867

IN CANADA
P.O. Box 609
Fort Erie, Ontario
L2A 5X3

YES! Please send me 2 free Harlequin Presents® novels and my free surprise gift. After receiving them, if I don't wish to receive anymore, I can return the shipping statement marked cancel. If I don't cancel, I will receive 6 brand-new novels every month, before they're available in stores! In the U.S.A., bill me at the bargain price of $3.80 plus 25¢ shipping & handling per book and applicable sales tax, if any*. In Canada, bill me at the bargain price of $4.47 plus 25¢ shipping & handling per book and applicable taxes**. That's the complete price and a savings of at least 10% off the cover prices—what a great deal! I understand that accepting the 2 free books and gift places me under no obligation ever to buy any books. I can always return a shipment and cancel at any time. Even if I never buy another book from Harlequin, the 2 free books and gift are mine to keep forever.

106 HDN DZ7Y
306 HDN DZ7Z

Name	(PLEASE PRINT)	
Address	Apt.#	
City	State/Prov.	Zip/Postal Code

Not valid to current Harlequin Presents® subscribers.

Want to try two free books from another series?
Call 1-800-873-8635 or visit www.morefreebooks.com.

* Terms and prices subject to change without notice. Sales tax applicable in N.Y.
** Canadian residents will be charged applicable provincial taxes and GST.
 All orders subject to approval. Offer limited to one per household.
 ® are registered trademarks owned and used by the trademark owner and or its licensee.

PRES04R   ©2004 Harlequin Enterprises Limited

eHARLEQUIN.com

The Ultimate Destination for Women's Fiction

For **FREE online reading,** visit www.eHarlequin.com now and enjoy:

Online Reads
Read **Daily** and **Weekly** chapters from our Internet-exclusive stories by your favorite authors.

Interactive Novels
Cast your vote to help decide how these stories unfold...then stay tuned!

Quick Reads
For shorter romantic reads, try our collection of Poems, Toasts, & More!

Online Read Library
Miss one of our online reads? Come here to catch up!

Reading Groups
Discuss, share and rave with other community members!

For great reading online, visit www.eHarlequin.com today!

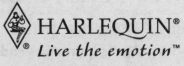

Coming Next Month

HARLEQUIN *Presents*

THE BEST HAS JUST GOTTEN BETTER!

#2487 THE RAMIREZ BRIDE Emma Darcy
Nick Ramirez has fame, fortune—and any girl he wants! But now he's forced to abandon his pursuit of pleasure to meet his long-lost brothers. He must find a wife and produce an heir within a year. And there's only one woman he'd choose to be the Ramirez bride....

#2488 EXPOSED: THE SHEIKH'S MISTRESS Sharon Kendrick
As the ruler of a desert kingdom, Sheikh Hashim Al Aswad must marry a respectable woman. He previously left Sienna Baker when her past was exposed—and he saw the photos to prove it! But with passion this hot, can he keep away from her...?

#2489 THE TYCOON'S TROPHY WIFE Miranda Lee
Reece knew Alanna would make the perfect trophy wife! Stunning and sophisticated, she wanted a marriage of convenience. But suddenly their life together was turned upside down when Reece discovered that his wife had a dark past....

#2490 AT THE FRENCH BARON'S BIDDING Fiona Hood-Stewart
When Natasha de Saugure was summoned to France by her grandmother, inheriting a grand estate was the last thing on her mind—but her powerful new neighbor, Baron Raoul d'Argentan, believed otherwise. His family had been feuding with Natasha's for centuries—and the Baron didn't forgive....

#2491 THE ITALIAN'S MARRIAGE DEMAND Diana Hamilton
Millionaire Ettore Severini was ready to marry until he learned that Sophie Lang was a scheming thief! Now when he sees her again, Sophie is living in poverty with a baby.... Ettore has never managed to forget her, and marriage will bring him his son, revenge and Sophie at his mercy!

#2492 THE TWELVE-MONTH MISTRESS Kate Walker
Joaquin Alcolar has a rule—never to keep a mistress for more than a year! Cassie's time is nearly up.... But then an accident leaves Joaquin with amnesia. Does this mean Cassie is back where she started—in Joaquin's bed, with the clock started once more...?

HPCNM0805